the dread south

HELL'S BELLES

and other stories

Sirius

HELL'S BELLES AND OTHER STORIES

STORIES OF THE DREAD SOUTH

SIRIUS

THE LAUGHING MAN HOUSE PUBLISHING

Hell's Belles and Other Stories

www.LMHPUB.com

Case Cover Design by Yune

Edited by Janus

For all the residents of Hell's Belles.
You will never get away from the words of the writer
who haunts you.

THE DREAD SOUTH

Blackjack + Moonshine
Funny Little Town
Gospel of the Cuckoo
Late Night Testament
The Devil Owns Primetime
A Great + Terrible Revival
Happy Face
House of Sinners
Abernathy
Hell's Belles (and Other Stories)
On Air with the Devil! (2026)

welcome to
HELL'S BELLES

There is blood mixed in the concrete that makes up the foundation of Hell's Belles. In the middle of nowhere, East Texas, you are likely to stumble across it. She only comes alive for the devil. She's his only love, keeping all his darkest discoveries locked behind steel doors, blinding the wandering and wayward with neon lights and drowning them in top shelf whiskey. The souls that he collects, she digests, a many-chambered extension of Gluttony's stomach. If you find this casino on your own, it is likely that you are already damned, and don't need the devil's help—or you're beyond it.

But since you're here, come inside and sit a spell. Have a drink at the bar and lose some money on the blackjack table. You're not alone, here. There are many other souls deteriorating all around you.

You might even see the devil, if he's looking for you.

Twice a day at 4:15, every light in the casino flickers. The air crackles with electricity and smells like burnt wiring, and the music goes silent. The slot machines stop whirring; no chips or cards hit the table. The interruption lasts for three full minutes, and then the lights are back on as if nothing ever happened. Some of the residents will tell you, 'it's a basement issue', but no one goes down into the basement. Especially not the devil. Whatever is down there, rumor has it, is something he does not wish to see.

OZIAS

go get 'em, killer

The first time he killed, Ozias waited for the guilt to hit him. He sat on his bathroom floor with his arms resting on his knees and hot, sticky blood soaking through the front of his shirt. All he could see of the dead woman in his bathtub was her arm, which was dangling over the side and leaking blood onto his obnoxious aqua-colored tile. He must have stabbed her sixty or seventy times, something like that, until his hand started cramping. He didn't even know why, if he was being completely honest with himself. Other than the fact that she had given him the opportunity, and he had seized it just like anyone else would have, in his position.

The guilt didn't come. Instead, as the minutes crept by, he was hit with a twang of panic. *What* was going to do with her body? His eyes scaled the shower curtain, which he could wrap her up in, but it was a clear one. He could always double-wrap the corpse in a tarp once he had her out of the bathroom, but then, what? His neighbors weren't good for much, but they were *nosy.* They would notice a nearly six foot man, who was mostly known for tending to his prize-winning hydrangeas, dragging a body out through his garage and tossing it in the trunk of his '67 white Mustang.

He should have planned this better.

He didn't even want to think about what it would take to get all that blood out of the bathroom. Borax, baking soda, and a few hours' on his knees scrubbing. At that point, was it even worth it?

Yes. The answer came rushing through him before he could even dismiss the thought. He shivered from his shoulders down to his toes while every muscle in his body tightened. *Yes,* it was worth it. Holding down her squirming body, feeling her writhe underneath his hand, exhaling the euphoria and *relief* that came with every thrust from his knife. He'd tuned out her screams, because that wasn't what he liked most. He liked how her blood made her blazing-hot skin slick. He liked how helpless she became, and how her fear tasted on the back of his tongue *(mostly like copper, the smell of her blood).*

But he had to clean the mess, if he wanted to do it again. His head spun a little as he grabbed the edge of the bathroom sink and pulled himself up from the floor. Order of operations— he had to dismantle the shower curtain, pull her body out of the bathtub, wrap her up and then drag her out...

Within thirty minutes, he had it all done, with her body waiting for him in the kitchen by the garage door. Ozias grabbed a wooden crate full of cleaning supplies out from under his sink and walked back into his bathroom to start scrubbing. Better to tackle that first, rather than let the blood congeal and dry. After that, he went upstairs to his second bathroom and took a shower, stuffing his dirty clothes into a trash bag and washing all the sticky, arterial blood off his chest and arms.

He couldn't do anything about the scratches on his arms. He picked a light brown cardigan to wear over a clean shirt and thanked God that it was encroaching on autumn.

He thought the guilt would come once he had to back his Mustang into the garage in order to load it up. He did that as quickly as possible, which didn't leave much time for any lingering doubts.

He cruised carefully out of his suburb, because a sleepless neighbor would surely notice if he peeled out of his driveway at nearly three in the morning. Once he was on the main road, he hit the gas and burned good Kentucky rubber.

The dump site was a brown river that stretched on for miles and was flanked by massive trees. Ozias kept his car running as he pulled the body out of his trunk and dragged it to the side of the bridge. He kept an eye out for any oncoming cars as he gripped the crinkled tarp in both hands and lifted, hauling the body over the side and watching it break the water like a rock, landing with a horrendous *slap and splash.*

He stood there for half a minute and waited, as if the body had a chance of bobbing back up to the surface. He didn't see anything, and the wind shaking the browning trees made him nervous. He slipped back into his car and fished between the seats for the unfinished carton of cigarettes he *knew* he'd stuffed down there. The nerves spread through his entire body, making his hands shake and his teeth chatter.

The car engine died. It stopped purring right as he yanked a slightly-crumpled cigarette from the mangled carton with his teeth. Ozias swore and turned the keys to the left, then to the right, cranking the Mustang so that it chugged and whirred, but didn't kick back to life. Ozias gave it a rest and pulled out his keys, taking a minute to light his cigarette and have a deep drag to calm his nerves. He counted to eight and then tried again with the keys. This time, the car started up, and he nearly shat himself in relief.

Until he turned his headlights on, and saw someone was standing right in front of him— close enough to touch the hood of the car, if they wanted to. Ozias' heart raced and sent his blood roaring through his ears. His first instinct was to run this person over. To tap them with the Mustang and watch them fly. He stuck his cigarette back between his teeth and slammed the gas pedal down to the floor, but his wheels only spun and went nowhere, like a radio-controlled card being picked up by its child handler.

The person in front of him smiled. Ozias assumed they were a man because of the broad shoulders and ungodly amount of chest hair, but he had been wrong before. Whoever it was, he was dressed all in white from his suit to his dress shirt, and the headlights lit him up like a beacon. From where he was standing, it was hard for Ozias to make out the fine details of his face. Half of it was obscured anyway from a plume of smoke that poured from the end of a burning cigar.

Ozias pulled his foot off the gas so his wheels stopped spinning. The stranger walked around to the driver's side window and leaned against the car, propped up on one arm his acrid smoke clouding the glass.

Tanned knuckles rapped on the window. Ozias took a deep breath and cranked it down. He had nothing to worry about, he reasoned with himself. He was the one knew how to kill. *He* was the dangerous one. Whatever this man had seen, it could all easily be erased with the edge of a knife.

He finally got the window low enough and the man slid a pair of round lavender sunglasses down his nose. He had the most staggering blue eyes that Ozias had ever seen, and just looking into them made him feel a little colder.

"Come here often, handsome?" the man at his window asked. Ozias' stiff fingers twitched.

"Can I help you?" Ozias asked, keeping his response short to try and convey his disinterest in chit-chat. Not only that, but his tongue was moving a lot slower, and he still couldn't tear his eyes away from that penetrating blue gaze.

"Oh, don't mind me none. I just saw you and I *had* to know what you are all about." The stranger's hand slip through the open window and grabbed Ozias by the chin. Those blue, blue eyes became his entire world, drawing him in and swallowing him up in pupils like spreading drops of ink.

Ozias' tongue was completely still, like it had been pinned to the roof of his mouth. He protested with a sound, but even to his own ears it sounded weak.

"Oh, that's so interesting," the stranger purred. "You really, just, don't want to get caught, don't you? That's all you'd ask for." His words started to distort like Ozias' whole head was being held underwater. "Well, I think I can accommodate you there, handsome."

Ozias tongue no longer felt like it was ballooning behind his teeth. He gasped and turned his head while the stranger slid away, pulling his round lavender glasses back up over his eyes.

"Fuck me!" Ozias growled, spitting into his floorboard.

"Only if you ask nicely." The stranger grinned and flashed a sharp gold canine. "Move over, honey bunch, I'll drive."

"Like hell; this is my car."

"You've got cops on your tail, 'like hell' is how you're going to want to get out of here."

At that, Ozias blanched. *Cops?* But, how would they know? One of his neighbors must have said something, seen him and gotten suspicious, phoned it in while standing at their window while he pulled out of his driveway...

While his head was still spinning, the stranger opened the door and Ozias crawled into the passenger seat. The car revved loudly without the stranger even touching the gas pedal—or maybe Ozias just imagined it that way. The stranger's grin widened with the engine's purr.

"What's your name?" Ozias asked, still feeling dazed.

"You can call me Bee, if that suits you."

"What if it doesn't?" Ozias asked, just to be difficult.

"Then tough shit, I suppose, I don't respond to much else." Bee barely tapped the gas pedal, it seemed, and the car went flying along the bridge. Ozias' hand slammed against the passenger-side door and he gripped the handle, grinding his teeth to try and keep from swearing.

Bee laughed, a laugh that sounded like a bobcat screaming, and placed his cigar back between his teeth. He only had one hand on the wheel and was spinning the slick leather around his palm like a kid in a teacup ride. "Lighten up, Ozzy baby, I'll get you home in one piece."

"How do you know my name?" Maybe *he* was a cop. In fact, the longer Ozias thought about it, that made more sense than anything. He'd let a cop into his car, and now they were probably driving down to the station where they would book him and lock him up forever. And he couldn't do anything about it, not at this speed. Taking out the driver would have sent the whole car spinning and Ozias would never kill again, either way.

"I know everything. Except I don't know how to keep the vanilla wafers in a banana pudding from going soggy. That's top-tier devilry and out of my jurisdiction."

If Ozias clenched his jaw any harder, he was going to start swallowing his own teeth.

"If you don't pull over this car and let me out, I'm going to pistol-whip you until you spray brains," he said, although his lacking tone did not match his threat.

That laugh again, louder than before.

"If you want me to stop driving, I will." Bee took his hand off the wheel and Ozias' heart did a flip. He reached out in a panic to take hold of the wheel himself and Bee swatted his hand away before re-taking control.

"What are you?" Ozias asked. Between the smoke, the noise, and the turbulence, all of his reason felt like it was leaking out of his ears.

"I'm your dream come true, baby," Bee said. "I'm your only way out of this mess. You did a number on that broad back there, and you want to do it again, don't you?"

Ozias made a face at the word 'broad'. "I work alone," he said flatly.

"Uh huh, and you'll die alone too. Come on now, be serious and answer the question."

"I want to do it again," Ozias said, this time without any hesitation. "I liked the way it felt. I keep waiting to feel guilty, but I don't, and maybe I won't." He wasn't sure why he was sharing any extra details. They seemed to just come spilling out of him.

"You won't," Bee said. Ozias wasn't sure whether that was meant to be reassuring. Bee kept going. "Maybe late at night, when you're laying in bed and you're sweating over getting caught—those are the hours when you might feel a pang of regret. But it isn't true guilt, and if you know that you're *not going* to get caught,

14

then who knows if you'll even get that far?" Orange sparks flew as he ashed his cigar out the window.

"How can you know that?" Ozias asked, which was a ridiculous question in the face of someone who knew his name without even asking, and his crime without even being in the room.

"Because your run-of-the-mill killers are a dime-a-dozen, but you're special, baby. You've got franchise potential. You could go nationwide. No night sweats, no terrors, nothing but the drive to keep on doing what you love because you're good at it. I can take away the consequences, make it so that you never, ever have to pony up for your actions."

"Why?" Ozias pressed. "Why would you?"

"Because I want to see what you do," Bee shrugged. "I think you're cute, it'd be a shame to see you hit the chair before you really got going."

Ozias leaned forward as much as he dared and dropped his head into his hands. "And what about you? What do you get?"

In the rearview mirror, Bee's smile spread.

"Well, Ozzy, it's all about give and take. You do a *lot* of taking, so you need to *give* a lot back." He rolled his cigar around between his fingers. "Every kill you make, I get to fuck you, I mean *really* fuck you, and I choose when it comes time

_____

to collect. Appetite for appetite, right? My hunger is as deep and empty as yours."

Ozias wasn't *completely* sure of what that last part meant, but he was starting to put the pieces together. And, well, there were worse bargains to be made. If this man—well, he wasn't a man, was he? He was a devil, if Ozias had ever seen one—could really follow through, then that meant Ozias could fill his need, his *hunger*, without any consequence. Gorge himself until he was sick. And at the end of the day, all Bee wanted from him in exchange was a little box? Bee might have been deranged, but he was handsome as hell. It wasn't a hard bargain.

Ozias dropped his scrutinizing gaze down to Bee's lap and gave it an ounce more thought.

"All right," he said at last. "Appetite for appetite."

Bee let out a howl like a coyote, while the car flew so fast that the trees and the sky began to blend.

The wheels were smoking when they stopped. Ozias got out of the car and ran his hand worryingly over the frame, checking for any dents or scratches.

"Is my car immune to harm, as well?" he asked dryly.

"*Consequences,* not harm," Bee corrected him. "Not that I'm eager for you to have any bumps or bruises, but it's best to clarify."

"Fair enough," Ozias said. He pulled himself away from his baby and dragged his garage door shut, unable to stop himself from looking both ways out of habit to see if there were any spying faces peering through their windows.

The house smelled *clean* when he walked in. It was the bleach and the borax, he was vaguely aware, but it was odd when he had been expecting blood and rot. He caught Bee looking around, hands in his pockets as he ambled across the living area and headed straight for the bedroom. He didn't beckon, but Ozias followed him anyway.

Ozias wished, belatedly, that his room was in better shape. The sheets of his full-size bed were rumpled and there were clothes on the floor. Posters of some of his favorite bands; Poison, Oingo Boingo, and Def Leppard among others, were plastered to the wall and the slanted ceiling above a turntable with two disorganized soda crates full of vinyl on either side. Bee stood in front of the turntable and dropped the needle onto the record that was already on top. Oingo Boingo's *'Who Do You Want to Be'* started playing and Ozias walked over, his tongue flicking nervously over his bottom lip.

"It's the new album," he said, although the tension was palpable and his attempt at conversation was not helping.

"I dig it," Bee said. He glanced over at Ozias and those blue eyes crawled up and down his entire body. "You don't look like a killer."

Ozias's face turned hot and he pushed a hand through his hair. "I'm not a coordinate-your-wardrobe-to-the-event sort of gay," he said.

Bee laughed. It was a softer sound than before. More human. He moved closer to Ozias and snaked an arm around his waist, bringing one hand to rest against his back before drawing him in and closing the remaining distance between them. "You could do without a few layers." He picked up the edge of Ozias' cardigan and slid it off his shoulders. It joined a pair of abandoned pajama pants on the ground and was quickly followed by his shirt, then the swathe of ace bandages he wore wrapped around his chest. Ozias stood there, feeling entirely exposed even though he was still half-dressed. There were chill bumps on his arms that raced up to his shoulders and his nipples stood erect from the apple-sized endowments on his chest.

Bee cupped Ozias' chest with his large, hot hands and pinched his nipples, just hard enough to draw out a gasp.

Suddenly, Ozias felt like he was trying to swallow around a tack.

"That's beautiful," Bee said with a brush of admiration over his thick, deep Southern accent. "You're damn fine, killer."

Ozias didn't know what to say. He let Bee pull him over to the bed and crawled back towards his pillows to better spread himself out, watching as the devil stripped his white blazer and his shirt, leaving only his golden cross necklace against his bare chest. The devil crawled towards him, taking hold of Ozias' pants by the belt loops and working them down his hips. Ozias trembled a little bit when his boxers slid off with them. He had felt exposed before, now he was completely *vulnerable.*

'Like the woman in the bathtub,' was his thought, and it felt ironic.

Bee placed one searing hand against the inside of Ozias' thigh and pushed his legs apart. Bee's head dove and Ozias yelped, panic jolting his chest as he grabbed the devil's hair without thinking.

"Wait! Stop! I mean, hold on, I'm sorry." His breath came out in little gasps. "I'm sorry, I just, I need a minute."

Bee's head came back up and he propped his elbow on top of Ozias' knee. "Second thoughts?" he asked.

"No, no." Ozias was dizzy, and he wanted to die at the same time. "I just...need to take it slow. I haven't, I've not...ever."

"Never?" Bee raised an eyebrow. "Well, I guess I'm not surprised." He watched Ozias from behind lavender lenses. "Take your time. I'm patient."

Ozias couldn't help but smile at that. If anything, it was half-embarrassment, half shyness from being so turned on. He put his hands over his face and tilted his head back, peering through his fingers at the ceiling until he collected himself. Pete Burns stared down at him, and he finally gathered the courage to nod.

"Keep going," he said. The next thing he knew, Bee was breathing against his cunt, and the devil's tongue slid over the outside—three up-and-down, long strokes before going deeper. Ozias's entire body shivered and he melted into the bed, lowering his hands to put them back in Bee's hair. The devil's tongue stretched him open, going deeper than he thought possible while being almost unbearably hot. Bee held his thighs apart until they were stretched to their limit and kept licking, flicking his tongue over Ozias' clit and sending electrical pulses of pleasure rocketing up his spinal cord.

Ozias had given himself several orgasms, but the one that started building was a new kind. It was tight across his belly and lit every nerve ending at once. He couldn't decide whether he wanted to scream for the devil to stop or beg him to keep going, but either way, he knew he wasn't going to avoid cumming for much longer.

Right at the precipice, Bee removed his tongue and came up to claim a kiss. Ozias almost screamed in frustration but took the kiss eagerly, holding Bee's face while tasting himself on his mouth. Bee pushed three fingers inside of him, going all the way down to the rings. Ozias's strangled moan staggered out and he writhed, grinding down on Bee's hand before his fingers left, also, and was replaced by the head of his cock.

Ozias grabbed hold of Bee's hips, pulling him to try and get the devil inside of him as quickly as possible. Bee hovered just outside of entering, waiting for what, Ozias didn't know. Ozias writhed, tormented by the presence of what he suddenly wanted so badly, but Bee's hand on his belly kept him from getting any closer.

Then, without warning, Bee plunged into him. Ozias screamed in pleasure and sank his nails into Bee's shoulders, hanging onto him as the devil speared him all the way through. Bee rocked his hips back and then thrust again, and again, fucking Ozias into the mattress so that his whole world was just a flurry of colors and sensation and vague, blaring music.

Ozias didn't last long, he couldn't. Bee pulled the orgasm out of him like he was yanking Ozias' soul out by the roots. He dug his nails deeper into the devil's shoulders as he came, clenching around that thick, pulsing cock that filled him so well, like it was *made* just for him.

Bee pulled out and hot, slick cum splattered all over Ozias' thighs and his cunt. He didn't even care, with his world still spinning above his head.

Finally, Bee pulled back. Ozias sat up a little and glanced down. There was blood on his sheets, and on the devil's cock.

"I'm sorry," he said, mortified. "I'm so sorry."

"Why?" The devil tossed him a stray blanket, presumably to wipe down with. "It's not the most blood you've spilled tonight."

Ozias swallowed the stubborn, imaginary tack lodged in his throat and stuffed the blanket between his legs. "Appetites," he muttered.

Bee flashed him a grin. "Both sated," he said. "At least for tonight."

A man sits at the bar with the remains of his head in a Halloween bucket, a plastic orange pumpkin like a cheap off-brand imitation of the Headless Horseman. He wears a cape around his shoulders with the collar and shoulders obviously drenched, but the black and red satin doesn't show blood very well. He has a tall beer in front of him, the best that the casino can offer him, but there's no way for him to drink.

GENE
the sad-sack ghost

"*SPECTACULAR NIGHT FRIGHTS OF THE UNDERGROUND*' had been on the side of the road just off of US 80 for over 25 years, and never once had Gene paid the rent on time. In fact, if he could go back in time and say anything to his younger self, it would be to thank that son-of-a-bitch and buy him a drink for setting the golden standard. Because now that Gene was closing in on fifty, he didn't pay the rent *at all.* The check was somehow always lost in the mail, or it arrived unsigned and he had to go down to the office (but never managed to get there). He couldn't imagine how embarrassing all that would be if he had been prompt from the word 'go' as a youth.

The landlord kept threatening to shut him down any day now. *'I'm putting this property up for sale. As soon as there's a sniff from a buyer, Coyle, you're out.'* Which, of course, Gene just had to laugh about. For one thing, there was nothing you could do *but* laugh. You had to have a sense of humor about these things. For another, what hard-up corporate piece of shit was going to look at a run-down shack held together with tobacco resin and a wish and slam fourteen grand down on the table? The customers just weren't coming anymore, that's what Gene kept telling his landlord. There was no mystery in their hearts, no wonder in their eyes. People didn't have whimsy, or whatever the hell. Now they just wanted clubs and synthesizers and powdered nose candy. Rock and Roll had completely killed the haunt industry, and he would attest to that with his whole chest.

Leggdon didn't care. That old parasite in a thrifted suit. Leggdon just wanted to retire early and offload the last few crappy buildings he owned onto some poor sod. He didn't care about the art. Although he was quick enough to tell Gene, *'The customers aren't coming because you don't have anything to see.'*

And that couldn't have been farther from the truth. Of course, *SPECTACULAR NIGHTS FRIGHTS OF THE UNDERGROUND* was no longer in its prime—but shit, neither was Gene. Did he deserve to get knocked in the head with a wrecking ball because of that? He used to hire scare actors, *real* people, not those shitty animatronics. Now, those were the good times, when they were all just a bunch of goofy twenty-somethings messing around in costumes and making middle-aged men clutch at their chests while their middle-aged wives clutched at them. There was nothing worth taking too seriously in those days. They weren't rolling in dough, but they were making money doing a whole lot of nothing-really. But then the actors got other jobs, the kind with benefits, and got married and had kids and just moved on with their lives. Gene kept going, but he was hiring college kids to fill in the gaps, and they weren't worth two spit-shined nickels rubbed together. Eventually, animatronics became the name of the game because they didn't call out and they didn't give him any lip, either.

Animatronics were expensive to maintain, so he only got a few good years out of them before they all started breaking down. At first, he used that to his advantage, figuring that being sort-of broken added to the creep-factor. But then they were all the way broken, not just sort-of, and he hung onto them as expensive lawn ornaments. He tried to breathe new life into the place with mystery bits and bobs of junk he uncovered from trade shows and estate sales, but nothing really threw *pizzazz* back into the old place. The glory days were gone, but he was still there.

Now, at forty-nine and a half, he still played the role. He opened up his costume trunk every morning and shook out the same dusty Dracula cape he'd donned for years while knocking the dents out of his felt top hat. It was commitment that got you places in life, and he was nothing if not absolutely loyal to his part. It would all come back around, eventually. You never *stopped* being great. People just started to look past you.

People were as bad as parakeets. Always wanting *shiny*, never wanting *substance*.

He sat on top of a stool in front of his cash register, his favorite spot in the whole joint, and chewed on the end of a toothpick while he counted out dimes and nickels on top of the counter. The jar they came from had a handwritten *'Animal Shelter Donations'* sign taped to the front. But he figured, hell, he'd been called a dog plenty enough to justify it.

Besides, he was jonesing for a beer, *badly.* He didn't care if it came in a bottle thicker than his forearm and was the color of piss, he wanted it. He'd been without for a day and a half, waiting for the residuals from that radio show he'd done three and a half years ago to come in so he could get some more. And now he couldn't wait any longer. It was either count coins, or he was going to start sniffing the isopropyl stuff in the bathroom.

The sound of the bell chiming above the front door nearly sent him backwards off his stool. Gene had only a collective three seconds to gather up his wits and push out the greeting that he'd had down pat since '64.

"Greetings, foolish mortal!" He grabbed the sides of his cape and flung his arms out, still seated, but cutting a rather imposing figure in his mind. "Do you dare to enter the house of SPECTACULAR NIGHTS AND FRIGHTS OF THE UNDERGROUND? Does it chill you to the bone to venture where none have gone before you and *survived?*"

The man in front of him smiled in a way that could only be described as *wolfish* and lit a cigar right where he stood. Immediately, Gene didn't like the look of him. White slacks, slicked back black hair, and round purple sunglasses (Gene had a pair of sunglasses just like that, he'd had them since Woodstock, this putz was poser). He was too tan, too chesty, too hairy—what porn set had he wandered off from? It was downright obscene, honestly. There were *laws* in Texas about not letting your nipples show and this guy had them jutting against his purple cotton dress shirt like it was twenty degrees outside in the middle of June. If he'd had one on hand, Gene would have tossed him a bra.

Gene was a feminist, God knew, burn the bra and all that, but he had standards. There was just something about this cat he didn't like.

"Hey there," the poser said. "You've caught me. I'm ready to be thrilled and chilled."

Gene deflated with a huff and lowered his arms to his side. "This ain't no *Rocky Horror Picture Show,* toots. Come on, now, have you ever been truly *terrified?*"

The poser shook his head. Go figure, honestly.

"Well, prepare yourself!" Gene tapped the register. "What lies beyond this curtain is not for the weak of heart or the faint of stomach. You will see all manner of wonders both great and terrible, and you will not know where next to direct your eyes. There will be no shielding yourself from the..." he trailed off, getting distracted while looking for the printed pamphlet that gave the full run-down. "...The...hm. Anyway. That's $29.95."

One of the poser's black eyebrows shot up, but he was still smiling. "A handsome fee. It must be wondrous."

"Worth every dime," Gene wagged a finger in his direction. "A good hour of entertainment if you walk real slow. Don't cheap out now, when you're one breath away from—*oh thank fuck.*" He yanked the pamphlet out from where it had gotten wedged underneath the register. "These shits are expensive to print."

The poser took another puff of his cigar and set his checkbook on the counter. That thing was oiled leather and looked brand new. The cheques were crisp and clean and didn't look like they'd been scratched through, not once. Gene had to catch himself staring and stop himself from salivating at the sight.

"Tell me something," the poser said. "How far is $29.95 going to get you?"

"Excuse me?" Gene's ears were too busy buzzing.

"I think it will buy you a few beers, maybe a halfway decent supper. It's been a while since you've treated yourself to anything other than that little diner up the way, hasn't it?"

Suddenly, Gene's mouth was dry. He looked up at the man, but all he was met with was cornflower blue eyes barely concealed by round lavender lenses.

"What do you know about that?" Gene asked, attempting to deflect while honestly *wondering.*

The poser shrugged and clicked his pen that was sleeker than a bullet. "How much, then, for you to drink yourself to death? I'm thinking a solid C-note. Clean and fair."

Gene tried to swallow, but the complete lack of moisture made it nearly impossible. He was a fish out of water, flopping around and gasping for air, except he was perfectly still, still clutching the pamphlet in his now-trembling hand. What was happening to him? And what was this guy on about?

He had to be some kind of stalker, talking about Gene's dinner habits. Or worse, he was from the government.

"But then," the poser continued, clicking his pen again. "I bet that I could turn this around, and offer *you* something for far less, that is worth far more."

Oh God, he was a *fucking salesman.* That was worse than the goddamn government. Gene slammed the cash register drawer shut.

"I'm not interested in buying anything," he said. "No religion, no vacuums. I've got all the carpet cleaner I need. So, unless you're here for a scare, I'm going to need you to shoo. I've got real customers to take care of."

The poser laughed. "Oh, yeah? Well, please, don't let me hold up the line." He stepped aside, as if to allow a flow of people standing behind him to clamor towards the register. But of course, there was no one.

Gene ground his teeth. The longer this guy stood there, the more he got Gene's hackles up—and if he didn't think there was still a chance of squeezing some cash out of this poser, he'd tell him again to get lost. With conviction, even.

"All right, smarty-mouth-sassy-pants," Gene relented instead. "You can pay me forty dollars to listen to your sales pitch. $29.95 for the horror show and the extra is for the Advil I'm going to need after hearin' you jaw all afternoon."

The amusement melted off the poser's face about as quickly as it settled there. He touched the edges of his sunglasses like he was going to slip them up, but then he stopped himself and just adjusted them on the bridge of his nose.

"I caught wind of you miles away," the poser said. "You reek of desperation and I know you'd make a damn fine meal, so I'll consider you worth my bother up to a point. But when I leave, this is all going up in flames." He made a broad gesture. "And you can go with it, dead or alive."

Gene opened his mouth and then shut it again, feeling all the blood draining out of his face.

"What's your game?" he asked. He had a telephone, yes, but it wasn't connected to anything. Pick up the receiver and you'd get only a dead line. He'd installed some kind of panic button under the counter, but that hadn't worked in years, either. He was all alone, him and this guy he didn't like. Which had been bad enough before things escalated to threats of murder.

"A second chance at youth," the poser said. "That's all you've wanted for a while, isn't it? You're stuck on this schtick because it's all you have left from the days when anyone gave a damn about you."

Harsh, maybe, but Gene couldn't deny that there was a grain of truth to that. He scrubbed his hands down the front of his pants, unable to resist a bit of snark for a response.

"Well, yeah...I'd like that and a million dollars, if you have it to spare." He sneered.

The stranger slammed his palm down on the counter. He wore a gold ring on every finger, and they all winked at the same time.

"Dead, or alive," the stranger repeated each word deliberately as if Gene's skull was too thick to let them through the first time. "This is the last chance I am going to give you to choose how it will go."

Gene licked his lips and held up his hands. "Okay, okay," he said. "Sheesh, all right. Didn't mean anything by it, can't take a joke..." He trailed off, muttering, then rocked back and forth on his stool while he gave it some thought. "So...I get my youth back, then what—I live forever?"

"You only live to the end of your natural life," the stranger said. "I can't do anything about that."

"Fair, okay." Gene stopped rocking and drummed his hands against his thighs. "What do you get out of it? My soul?" He flinched even as the word escaped, not trying to trigger another meltdown just because he was incapable of being serious.

"On toast," the stranger said. "Normally, I don't bother with the details with someone like you, who won't get it. But yes, at the end of your days, I am going to split open your ribcage, spoon out your heart, and eat your yellow-jelly soul."

Gene grimaced. "What a way to go." He gave the stranger another once-over. "You know, if you're the real deal, I think you'll be surprised. I looked a lot like you, back in the day, 'course my hair was thicker." He ran his hand over his own thin, straw-like hair. "I guess you could say whatever you are, I'm the original."

The stranger snorted and took another drag off his smoldering cigar before he straightened. "If you need me, just call," he said. "My name is Bee."

"I didn't ask for your life story," Gene said. He popped open the register to fish for a blank piece of paper, taking *just call* very literally. "Write down your number, so that I..." His words stopped dead in the air when he looked up. Bee was gone, and Gene was left standing there with a torn piece of an envelope in one hand and a dying pen in the other.

ene finished counting out his nickels and dimes and, by the time he was out the door and headed to the convenience store, the conversation with the wannabe pornstar had already faded enough to feel like a dream. He was sweating bullets when he pulled open the heavy door, and the AC flash-froze his sweat so that the droplets stuck to his forehead.

"Morning, Ringo," he called out to guy standing behind the counter while he made a beeline for the coolers. Those white plastic shelves, brighter than a dentist's smile when lit up with an almost blue fluorescent light, were a sight for sore eyes. Gene reached in and grabbed the first 40 of beer he laid eyes on by the neck. He kept a death-grip on it with one hand while the other fished down in his pocket for his coins that jingled and jangled as they smacked against his thigh.

"Jesus, you wouldn't believe the morning I've had," Gene said as he set the 40 onto the counter. He poured a handful of dirty silver coins right next to it and then wiped his hand off on his shirt. "That should be a dollar. Can I get a pack of Pall Malls?"

Ringo didn't immediately respond. He turned around and grabbed one of the red packs of cigarettes from the shelf behind his head, and then when he turned back, he said, "I need your ID."

Gene guffawed in his face. "Are you pulling my leg? You know I turn fifty next year." He furrowed his brow when Ringo's expression didn't move. "Come on, man."

Ringo shook his head. "ID," he said. "Or don't waste my time, kid."

Kid?! Gene's heart skipped a beat and he stepped back from the counter. "I don't have my

ID," he said. He didn't even know where it was. Last he'd seen it was stuck to the floorboard of the old Cab he'd bought, back when *'GHOSTLY HOSTED CAB RIDES'* were going to be a thing.

"Come back when you have it." Ringo, who wasn't usually such a hard-ass, grabbed the 40 and the cigarettes and set them behind the counter. Gene's dirty pile of nickels and dimes still sat there, sinking as the coins started to slide.

"Okay, okay." Gene went back just long enough to snatch up the coins and throw them back down into his pocket. "Whatever. You're the boss." He ran out of there with his heart still pounding. In fact, he felt like he was going to have a goddamn heart attack.

Once he was outside, Gene paused, leaning over just a little and resting his hands against his thighs. He was used to ignoring pain, but the sudden absence of it was what forced his attention back to his own body. His back didn't hurt, and his knees didn't ache, even though he had walked all the way from his place. Now, back in the day, Gene had walked all over Kingdom Come and rarely felt the burn. Once he hit middle-age, that had turned into a different story. Except now, he was fine.

Gene turned his head to get a glimpse of himself in the store window. Between the thick metal bars, the dark glass reflected the face of a young man with frazzled, curly brown hair and a thin mustache that ended in two wispy circles. He couldn't remember the last time he'd had so *much* hair, and maybe it was just the window, but he could hardly see his scalp through it.

"Hot holy balls!" he shouted out loud. Gene straightened up completely and looked again, stepping closer to the window and completely neglecting the fact that Ringo could *probably* see him from the other side. Gene pressed his fingertips into his cheeks and dragged them down towards his jaw before releasing, watching the skin bounce back up like it was made of silly putty.

"That guy wasn't fucking around." He started jogging backwards, still talking to himself while watching his own retreating figure in the window. "You look good, Gene, I mean *holy shit* you look good." He rotated on his heel and slowed to a walk as he reached the road. Just because his heart wanted to break out in a run didn't mean he was going to actually put his body through all that. "What are we going to do, now? I mean with all this time. With all this energy."

Even as he mulled it over aloud, he knew exactly what he was going to do.

The Bat n' Bull was an old saloon-style bar that had been converted into a goth club, but the owner fancied himself a real cowboy who also collected bones. He and Gene went way back, but Gene didn't even bother seeking him out for a friendly 'hello' when he walked through the door. He had a feeling that his old pal wouldn't recognize him, anyway, so there wasn't much point.

Besides, Gene had more important things on his mind. He'd spent the afternoon laundering his cape, digging his fake teeth out of the bottom of his junk drawer, and peeling his cracked ID off the bottom of his failed Cab scheme. The ID was expired, but with a little restoration magic (or, rubbing off the expiration date), it was good as new. At least it would suffice for one night.

The second Thursday of every month, *The Bat n' Bull* held a Count Dracula look-a-like contest. The first few months of its inception, Gene had competed every time, because his Dracula was *immaculate*. His cape was real black-and-red satin and he'd rigged with an

Elizabethan collar, paying tribute to Bela Lugosi but with his own touch. He used to wear a wig, but this time, he'd just slathered black dye all over his natural hair and combed it back. He felt like that added a layer of authenticity most of these other bozos couldn't produce, and a little face powder helped cover up the black streaks that swept across his forehead.

That wasn't everything, of course. There was a hand-embroidered corset he'd ordered from a woman who only did wedding gowns, but had made a special exception for him because she understood his vision. It didn't fit as well as it used to, but he left the back unlaced and covered it with the cape. No one could tell. He still was leagues above all the other competitors who looked like they'd just walked out with whatever was on sale at the Halloween store.

He'd never won, not once. Which really said something about his friend who ran the joint. But this time, he *would,* and he would take home the $30 cash prize they offered. That would get him a six-pack of beer, a nice steak dinner, and a couple packs of cigarettes to enjoy on his porch. And if someone offered him a bump while he was here, well—he wouldn't be mad.

The red and blue lamps inside the club were the only lights available once he got up the stairs that led to the dance floor. Near the stage, a few weirdos in their capes and cheap fangs were already gathered, like they didn't know where else to go while they waited to be called. They were kids, and he was an old hat at this. Even though he for damn sure didn't *look* like it anymore.

That thought made him a little giddy. Gene went down another three short steps that led into a separate section of the bar and jumped onto a stool. He slammed his cracked ID onto the counter and shouted, "I'll have an extra dirty martini," over The Cure's *Just Like Heaven* playing through the speakers.

The bartender looked at him, glanced down at the ID, and then nodded. She didn't even smile at him, good lord. She had an *attitude.* He was magnanimous about it, though, and turned away to look out across the club floor while she made his drink. When she set the glass on the counter, he just mouthed, "open a tab".

Thirty dollars. And he already knew what he was going to order. Steak with butter, corn, and mashed potatoes loaded down with gravy. His mouth watered just thinking about it. It wasn't all about the food, of course, there was a good level of *satisfaction* attached to his inevitable prestige. People had forgotten exactly *who* he was, how he was revered as a local legend and upstanding community member. They seemed all-too-willing to dismiss everything he did for the local goths and freaks to keep the scene going, but they would be reminded, even if he had to act as his own envoy. *Son of the Monster Keeper*, like a bad horror movie. And then the tagline *'OR IS HE?'* That really made his toes tingle.

His martini wasn't nearly as dirty as he would have liked it, but he sucked it down anyway. Gene turned around on his seat and set the empty glass back on the bar, snapping his fingers to get the bartender's attention.

"Hey, toots!" He leaned over a little. One more before the contest just to give him a boost of courage. Then he'd get out a good piss, and he'd be ready for the stage. His hands trembled only a little, and he figured that was just regular show nerves. Even though all he'd have to do was stand up there with a couple of yokels and be the best one. That was gonna be a piece of cake.

It was a different bartender, this time, who turned around and answered. She had long blonde hair and glasses that took up half her face, but despite the ugly-ass red frames, he recognized her immediately.

And then he had to wonder, *why* did his old pal, his best friend for over a decade, hire his ex-wife to work behind the bar? Talk about disrespect and talk about *gall*.

Gene almost fell off his seat getting up. He grabbed the edges of his cape and threw the hem back to keep himself from tripping over it. Cheryl, the woman he'd wasted three good years of matrimony on, was just staring at him like she had just stepped on a tack.

"Well, hi, Gene." She grabbed his abandoned glass. "Did you want something?"

"*No!*" Gene jabbed a finger in her direction. "*You're* not supposed to be here! What the *hell are you doing here?*"

"Making a steady paycheck," Cheryl said, tapping the edge of the glass. "I think that's more than I ever did with you, Gene."

"Oh, can it," he snapped. "Are you having plenty of orgasms, too? Did you have to go and *fuck* my best friend to get this job?"

Her expression went from discomfort to mortification, and he was at least a little satisfied about that. "Jesus, Gene," she lowered her voice. He could barely hear her over the music. "Do you have to be so loud? And no, I'm not messing around with Harry."

"Oh!" All Gene's blood went to his face and he rubbed it with both hands. "Sure, okay." He took another step back, almost delirious in his attempt to escape as quickly as possible. "Then he'll understand completely when I find his ass and remind him of all the things you did to me, and why you *shouldn't* be here! You have no goddamn right! I belong here! This is *my* space!"

"Gene, please." She looked embarrassed, as she should have been. "How much have you had to drink today?"

"You aren't even supposed to recognize me!" Gene almost screamed. "I don't know how you even recognize me!"

"I don't know what you're talking about," she said, and she sounded a little desperate. "Sit down, let me get you some water. You're acting..."

Gene clenched the sides of his cape. "I don't want *dick* from you," he said. "You ruined my fucking life. Get away from me!" He took another step back. "Get away, and stay away! And start emptying out those tip jars, because your ass is going to be unemployed before I walk out of here!"

His ankle hit the short steps leading up to the dance floor and he tumbled backwards. Gene hissed and scrambled back up, sprinting towards the dance floor and then staggering out into the open. The main area was quickly filling up with bodies, each one wrapped up in white fog that was being cranked out of a machine from near the DJ booth.

"Goddamn bitch!" he snarled, wiping at his own sweaty face. And if he smeared his makeup because of her, he was going to bust a capillary. "She has a lot of nerve, thinking she deserves to be in the same building, the same *town!* Thought she'd flown the coop long ago, caught the first sad sap loser scmuck out of here..." He wove his way through the crowd, still ranting, his eyes burning as he searched every corner for Harry, that two-faced son-of-a-bitch who had some serious explaining to do.

Every face was a blur. Gene passed a mirror hanging on a black, graffiti-covered wall and caught sight of his own face. For a split-second, all he could see was his scowling, sagging face smeared with black hair dye and his thinning hair looking sparser than ever, because black hair made him look like a greasy Italian. It was just an illusion, he knew, a trick of the light because his youth had been restored. He was hot, hotter than Cheryl had ever seen him, hotter than she could ever get again despite her best attempts at throwing herself at anyone who walked past.

Gene's next stride was just empty air. He didn't even realize how close he was to the staircase because of the fog, but now he found himself at the top of the steps, reaching out desperately for the wall. His cape twisted around his feet and he couldn't catch his balance, and Gene ended up tumbling down the stairs, hitting every other one with his head like a slinky.

Once he hit the bottom, Gene couldn't feel his legs. He groaned with his nose smashed against cement, and when he raised his head, hot blood gushed over his mouth and chin. He reached out and started clawing his way across the ground, dragging himself along his belly, swearing internally when he heard his cape snag over the ground. That was going to expensive to replace. He'd send the bill to Cheryl.

He didn't even know what he was really headed for. The road, maybe, to grab a taxi and get out of there. He didn't know how long it would take for the feeling to come back to his legs, but in the meantime, he had a hell of a lot of dignity to scrape back up. Nothing a beer or two couldn't fix.

White shoes interrupted his path. Gene hocked up a glob of blood on them.

"Lend a hand?" Gene asked, reaching up. He didn't even realize he *had* broken fingers until he saw them peeking out above his fingerless gloves.

A tan hand reached down and grabbed his, crushing it in its grip. The sudden squeezing sent more pain up Gene's wrist and to his shoulder, the only thing sharp enough to cut through the dull, throbbing pain in his head. Bee used his grip to haul Gene up a full inch above the ground.

"Low investment, high return," Bee's voice came from above his head. "That's something you should have been told from day one."

"What the fuck does that mean?" Gene spat again, disappointed when the splatter didn't land on the man's white slacks.

"You were set to expire, but at least this way, you didn't die alone at your empty register." The devil flashed a grin. "Though that would have been the cherry on top of your pitiful life's rap sheet."

"Fuck you!" More of Gene's blood burbled through his teeth. "I'm just getting started?"

"No, you're very done." Bee dropped his hand, and Gene hit the ground again. "I think the world has had enough of you."

"But I'm Gene Coyle!" he moaned. "The master of monsters and frights, I—"

The devil set his white shoe against Gene's forehead, leaning into it enough that pressure built up inside his skull. Orange embers fell from the end of his thick cigar and into Gene's eyes.

"I didn't ask for your life story," the devil in white said. One step, and all the pressure building up in Gene's head released with a burst.

There is a woman who walks through the casino, never resting, limping in designer heels on broken ankles. Shards of red and white glass sparkle like grisly uncut crystals from the deep lacerations in her face. She will stop to talk to you, and she will try to sell you her house. If you take her offer, you will be the one shambling in her place. Politely decline and move on.

NANCY

no 'i' in real estate

Nancy spread her thighs a little wider and pressed her back firmly against the granite countertop. The worst part about getting eaten out on such a narrow surface was that she couldn't figure out what to do with her arms. She didn't dare put them in Bea's hair or on her shoulders, because they had another house showing in thirty minutes and Bea was a professional, she wouldn't be happy about walking into a client's home looking all sexed-up. Nancy opted for locking her hands together and resting them above her own head, even if that meant they dangled off the edge just a little bit.

"Right there!" Nancy breathed, fighting the dual urges to both clamp her thighs around Bea's head and also shove her face away. "Right there, oh my God—fuck!"

Nancy's climax slammed into her hard enough to make her thighs shake and she rocked against Bea's face, sliding up and down the other agent's nose and mouth while Bea's hot tongue stroked her clit. Finally, Bea raised her head and smiled. Miraculously, only her wine-red lipstick was smudged.

"Oh my god," Nancy breathed again, wet and trembling and unable to convince herself to get up. She didn't want to do *anything* except take a fat bong rip and sleep for ten hours. Unfortunately, neither of those options were available to her on a Tuesday afternoon.

"Fix yourself up, sugar, we've got the Spector House showing in fifteen." Bea checked her pager and then turned to a hallway mirror to touch up her lipstick. Nancy finally sat up and pulled her pencil skirt down her thighs.

"My legs aren't going to hold me up," Nancy muttered.

"Sweetheart, you've got gorgeous legs. We'll stretch them out by walking since it's just down the road."

"It's eighty-five degrees," Nancy argued. "I'm not walking anywhere. My hair will go flat."

"High hair, highball bids? Is that the logic?" Bea walked back and dug a travel-sized bottle of hairspray out of her purse. "You messed up *my* hair."

"I'm sorry." Nancy slid off the counter and nearly crumpled as her heels wobbled. She grabbed the countertop and steadied herself before her ankles rolled. She felt a little bit like a newborn fawn as she walked over to the same mirror and checked her face. "How do I look?"

"Goddamn stunning, sugar. As always." Bea flashed another smile.

No matter what mood Bea was in, she had a smile like a bull shark about to drag a child underwater. She was pure Miami-gorgeous, with sleek black hair she kept swept back in a ponytail, suntanned skin made golden from hours spent walking up and down rich suburban sidewalks and exorbitant beach properties, and a white Gucci pantsuit that hugged every curve up to her enormous rack. She kept her blue eyes hidden behind a pair of purple-lensed Chanel sunglasses, which was

Nancy's only gripe. Too many times had she tried to swipe those sunglasses off Bea's face and nearly lost a hand in the process.

Today was their six-month anniversary as business partners. Although hand on a Bible, Nancy couldn't remember how or why they started working together. All she remembered was sitting in her car and crying outside of a gas station with no cigarettes, no hash, and no will to live. Her car back then had been a real piece of junk, not like her current Cadillac SUV, and there was so much trash piled up in her floorboards that it overflowed over the lip of her passenger seat.

Bea had knocked on her window and offered her a cigarette. The rest beyond that was a blur.

Bea's snapping fingers brought Nancy back around to the present.

"Tick tock, sugar," Bea said.

"I'm coming." Nancy grabbed her purse. "Are you really going to make me walk?"

"You need to have *some* kind of excuse for while you're all hot and sweaty." Bea grinned again and push her fingers through Nancy's hair, fluffing up her bangs. "You look like you went swimming."

"Steph is going to kill me," Nancy muttered.

"Is that eating you up inside?" Bea pulled a cigar case out of her purse as soon as they stepped out the door.

"Not as much as it should," Nancy admitted. "And I don't know why I can't just walk away. It's not like we're married, or anything."

"She's still taking care of your mom, isn't she?" Bea asked, clipping off her cigar's tip and tossing it into a bush.

"You're going to piss off this HOA," Nancy warned.

"I up the resale value just by being here, the HOA can piss off," Bea said. "Are you going to answer my question?"

"Yes, Stephanie still takes care of my mom," Nancy replied. "But it isn't like she has a job; well, she's been selling magazine subscriptions over the phone."

"But you're paying the bills," Bea pointed out. "So, she's keeping house, doing a little bit of work here and there on the side—sounds like she's too busy to blow you."

Nancy passed a hand over her eyes. "Jesus Christ."

"In-home care is expensive, I get it. And you're going to spend a fortune getting everything steam-cleaned if you ever decide to move. You might as well catch your breaks where you can."

"You can be a real cold bitch sometimes, Bea." Nancy scoffed.

"Cold heart, hot fingers." Bea winked. "Besides, hon, I'm not the one stepping out on my girlfriend just for kicks."

It was 9PM when Nancy returned home carrying a paper bag of fried chicken from a late-night spot down the road. Despite all the changes that had transpired over the last six months, the only thing that hadn't seen an upgrade was her mother's house. The three of them still occupied that single-level, three bedroom, two bath ranch-style atrocity that lurked on the outskirts of town. The carpet needed to be pulled up, the roof needed new shingles, and Nancy was pretty sure that the foundation was starting to bow. However, they didn't have a mortgage payment, and Stephanie was extremely vocal about not getting one until Nancy was 'a little more settled in' with her job.

The front storm door swung wide open with barely any prompting. Nancy was fishing for her keys when Stephanie appeared and pulled her inside.

"I *just* got your mother to sleep," Stephanie hissed. "I'd appreciate it if you didn't bang things around and wake her up."

"Sorry," Nancy whispered, holding up the bag. "I brought some dinner."

"I ate already." Stephanie moved past her, and Nancy followed. She only paused long enough to slip off her heels by the straps.

"I'm sorry I'm late," Nancy said, lifting her volume only a little once they were in the kitchen together. "We had three showings today..."

"You're always late, Nance." Stephanie sounded tired as she pulled the coffee pot from its burner and started making herself a cup. "Nine o'clock is really normal for you."

"I'm still sorry." Nancy collapsed into a chair and set the paper bag down. She thought about digging out some chicken, but suddenly she wasn't very hungry. "How was mom today?"

"Lively. Her meds weren't ready this morning so we had a difficult afternoon." Stephanie rubbed her face. "I didn't get any housework done."

"That's okay," Nancy said. "Did you make any sales?"

"No. Allow me to remind about my *difficult afternoon*." Stephanie added three spoonfuls of sugar into her cup and then a hefty drizzle of caramel dessert syrup.

"I'm sorry. It sounds like your day sucked." Nancy leaned over and pulled up one of her feet, massaging her aching sole through the thin hose. "Bea had me walking all up and down Magnolia..."

"I do *not* want to hear about Bea," Stephanie snapped. Nancy's eyebrows went up.

"Okay," she said. "Ouch. I mean, what's wrong with her? She's just my business partner."

"Right, and now you're home with me," Stephanie said. "And I think you should leave work at work." There was a harder undercurrent to her tone that Nancy couldn't decipher.

"All right, fine." Nancy dropped her foot and stood. Her knees were still shaky. If she thought too hard about it, she could still feel Bea's tongue darting between her legs. "I'm going to go take a shower."

"Before you go-" Stephanie walked over to the table and picked up the edge of a white business envelope. "You got some mail."

Nancy picked up the envelope and tore it open. The paper was pink and the letters at the top were bold, red, ***FINAL NOTICE!***. Her heart sank and she folded it up quickly.

"What is it?" Stephanie reached for the paper.

"Nothing, it's from the dealership," Nancy said. "I'll go over there tomorrow before work."

"Nancy!" Stephanie tore the notice from her hand and flipped it over. Her whole face turned the same color as the paper. "Jesus Christ, Nance, have you not been making your car payments?"

"I guess it kept slipping my mind. You always take care of the bills." Nancy's head start spinning and she couldn't make sense of the words, even when she took the paper back and read it all over again. All she could think, for some reason, was *'this isn't supposed to happen. It's not part of the deal'.*

"Yeah, except you told me specifically, *'I can take care of it, Steph, I'll pull the payments from the new bank account.'*" Steph's tone instantly plummeted to ice-cold depths of rage. "A bank account that I don't have access to, by the way. So, what have you been spending all your money on? See, *this* is why I said I didn't want to move! Because you're barely six months into this job and you're already getting your car repoed...!"

"Shut up, Stephanie! Just *shut the fuck up!*" Nancy grabbed the paper bag sitting on the table and threw it at her girlfriend. Stephanie sidestepped the bag and it hit the cabinet behind her. The bag burst and fried chicken flew everywhere.

"You're unbelievable," Stephanie said in a deceptively calm voice.

"This is wrong." Nancy held up the notice. "This was *not* supposed to happen! It is *not* part of it!"

"Part of *what?*" Stephanie pressed.

"I don't know," the dizziness was getting worse. "I'm going to talk to Bea about it. Bea is going to know."

"What does Bea know about your money that I don't?" Stephanie demanded.

"She just knows." Nancy started staggering towards the hallway. "She said that everything was going to be okay. That I wouldn't have to worry about anything ever again." Even as the words stumbled out of her mouth, she had no idea where they were coming from. It was like babbling something from a dream.

"Nancy, we need to talk!" Stephanie called after her, but Nancy didn't stop. She went into her bathroom and locked the door behind her, latching onto the edges of the sink and holding her head over the bowl.

Nancy heaved, but she didn't vomit. Her nose burned, which made her eyes teary, but nothing even welled up over the waterline. She raised her head to look in the mirror and was horrified by the sight of her own face. Her lipstick was smeared, her eyeliner was smudged, and every moussed strand of brown hair was limp and hanging around her shoulders. Her whole life was falling to pieces and apparently, she looked the part.

Nancy pulled a jar of cold cream down from the medicine cabinet and smeared it all over her face to break up the day's makeup. She ran a washcloth under some hot water and used it to wipe everything away. Then she stared at her bare face a little more, at her red-rimmed eyes and her swollen lips from where she'd scrubbed off that Avon lipstick that went on like paint and wouldn't budge.

A fly landed on her mirror, pacing a circle on little black feet.

She had to call Bea, but her phone was in the bedroom, and Stephanie was in the way.

Her girlfriend stood on the other side of the bathroom door. Nancy heard her breathing.

"Nance," Stephanie finally said. "Come out here and talk to me. Please?"

Nancy hesitated. "I have to make a phone call, Steph," she said. "I have to get this sorted out or...or I'm not going to be able to sleep."

She clenched her thighs and gripped the sides of the sink again. The memory of Bea's tongue was like getting smacked with a belt, and it kept coming out of nowhere. Every time it hit, her legs got weaker.

And she didn't know *why* she was still thinking about it during a time like this.

"Nancy, I'm really worried about you," Stephanie said. "And I think there's something off with Bea...with this whole thing, actually." She paused. "I don't think she's doing you any good."

For some reason, that set Nancy off. She unlocked the door and yanked it open.

"Bea *saved* me!" Nancy snapped, barely able to breathe from how much anger was balled up in her chest. "She gave me a job and she got me out of this house—this *godforsaken house* where I am otherwise stuck with you all day!"

The look on Stephanie's face made her *almost* regret her words, but neither of them could skate past the fact that she meant what she said.

"What did she promise you?" Stephanie asked quietly.

"I don't remember." Nancy grabbed the back of her own neck and dug her fingers into her skin. "That's why I have to call her."

Stephanie stepped aside and didn't say anything else. Nancy tore past her, racing for the bedroom where she grabbed the black cordless housephone from its cradle.

Nancy froze as soon as she had the phone in hand. Did she even have Bea's number? She ripped her pager off her belt clip and scrolled through, looking for any number that didn't ring a bell as a client. She finally found one, and then she dialed.

The phone rang three times before it finally picked up. "Hey, sugar," Bea's voice purred from the other end.

"Oh my god." Nancy's relief almost had her dissolving into tears. "Bea, I'm so sorry. I need to talk to you about..."

"About the deal?" Bea supplied.

"Yes," the word came out as a gasp.

"I don't like to give timelines for this very reason," Bea said. "They lead to all sorts of expectations."

"I don't understand," Nancy said. "And I don't know what's going on. I've got this notice from my...from my dealership that says my car is going to get repossessed and I...I don't know how that could happen because you said...you said that I wouldn't have to worry ever again."

"Is that what I said?" Even from the other side of the phone, Bea sounded like she was smiling. "I don't know, Nancy baby, I was on board until I realized how little you know about taking care of yourself. I don't think Stephanie's much better, mind you, but I also think you're doing her pretty dirty. And if this is where you are after six months, where do you think you'd be in a year? I don't really have the time, or the desire, to watch you dig this same hole."

It didn't feel real. None of this was real. "Bea, please," Nancy's voice broke. "I can't do this without you. I don't know what I'm doing when you're not there."

"I know, honey. It's not going to last much longer. Look behind you."

"Bea-!"

"Look *behind you,* Nancy."

Nancy turned with the phone still pressed to her ear. Stephanie stood in the bedroom doorway, tears leaving hot red streaks as they raced to her chin. Nancy reached out to her, but Stephanie turned and darted away. Nancy ran after her, still holding onto the phone.

"Stephanie!" Nancy's voice didn't even sound like it was coming from her mouth. Her mother called her name from the other room, but Nancy didn't answer. She was too busy trying to stop Stephane from grabbing the car keys off the table, but her girlfriend was too quick.

Stephanie didn't even stop to put on shoes. She ran out the front door and went straight for the Cadillac SUV. Nancy grabbed her wrist in another attempt to hold her back, but Stephanie flung her arm back and knocked Nancy in the face with her keys.

Nancy backed up and Stephanie climbed into the driver's seat. She was still crying as she backed up the car.

"Stephanie!" Nancy pressed the phone to her ear again. "Bea...Bea! Stephanie is leaving." She raised her voice, screaming at the car even though the windows were rolled up. "Stephanie is leaving! Good riddance, bitch! Ae you going to come move in with me, Bea?"

The line buzzed. Bea wasn't on the other end.

Nancy darted towards the end of the driveway, her pantyhose snagging on the stippled edges of the concrete. She hurled the phone at the car and it bounced off the windshield before flying back and hitting her in the nose.

Pain exploded through her skull and sent her reeling. Nancy clutched her face and fell forward, staggering to keep her balance, and then bright lights flooded her vision.

The front end of the car collided with her side, and Nancy was pulled under the wheels. Her legs and ribs cracked twice as the tires rolled over her, and then she was laying on the asphalt with blood pouring from her face, unable to feel any part of the lower half of her body.

The SUV stopped. Stephanie didn't get out to check on her. There was only a second's pause before the car started to back up, and then Stephanie must have hit the gas, because it rocketed back and rolled over Nancy twice more, then another two times as it sped onward and vanished down the street.

There were tire tracks with Nancy's blood that trailed off into the darkness. The disappearing taillights were the last thing she saw before she closed her eyes for good.

In the karaoke room, there is a singer who looks like a rockstar. They never sing, because their mouth is always full, cheeks stuffed to bulging with paper spilling out from their puckered mouth. They're blue and purple in the face, almost invisible underneath the lights that bathe the sad little carpeted stage where they stand. There are deep scratch marks around their mouth and down their throat where they have tried to claw the paper out, but it is never-ending. If they manage to pull any out, it is immediately replaced by more.

GRACE
baby stole my words

race sat with their ankles hooked around the legs of a tall barstool and tried not to look like they were about to throw up. It was hard, because of how acid kept surging up their chest and making them burp.

They tried to get it all out, now, because soon it would be their turn on the mic.

The woman on stage was nearing the end of her set—and *thank God*. Grace had heard just about of her sick crooning that sounded like a cat shitting out gumdrops and rainbows. Penny Dreadful, the artist, billed herself as a folk artist comparable to the likes of Fiona Apple and Tori Amos. Grace considered that to be far from true, even an insult to the other artists. But they couldn't say anything about it, at least not out loud, or they would be condemned as a 'jealous bitch'.

It wasn't the worst label in the world. It wouldn't prevent them from getting gigs. But it *might* prevent them from getting invited to cocktail parties and other social events where they could mingle and rub elbows with producers and other artists who actually *had* record deals. The one thing Grace wanted in the world was their face on a CD album cover.

Their agent sat on a stool next to them and claimed to be 'running numbers', although it seemed to Grace that he was just punching random digits into a calculator like a bored toddler. Grace chewed on the side of their tongue and actively fought against leaning over to take a look. Between the music, the clacking, and the nausea-heartburn combo, they were overstimulated as hell.

"Don't forget, we're going to be in Knoxville tomorrow," their agent said. "So after this, we're packing up and hopping on a plane. I've got your ticket in your bag."

"Thanks, Bee." Grace hunched over and stared at Penny intently. "Do we ever get a break?"

"No breaks unless you're dead." Their agent laughed like that was funny. "You wanted to be a big famous rockstar, right? *Without* 'sucking a barrelful of cock', those were your exact words."

"I know." Grace regretted that, almost as much as they regretted asking for help in the first place. "God. She can't sing worth a damn."

"Dreadful, some might say." Bee's grin widened.

"Oh, shut up." Grace rolled their eyes. They sat up again and rubbed their thighs, unable to stop their right leg from bouncing up and down. "I think this is her last song."

"Then you're going to get out there and blow 'em away, kiddo."

"I don't know about that." Grace gnawed on the inside of their cheek. "The crowd's responding well to her."

"She's doing covers. Everyone likes a cover. She did *Starman.* Even I liked that one."

"You're not helping," Grace snapped. Their other leg joined in the bouncing and now they felt like they were going to go sliding off the stool. "Original music never holds up in a crowd like this."

Bee's blue eyes gleamed behind his round purple sunglasses. "Original music? So you're doing '*Devil Caught My Roses*'?"

"Yeah." The nausea came back. Grace swallowed hard.

"That's a personal favorite of mine," Bee said. "That song's how you got me, kiddo. Even though your fingers were so sweaty they kept slipping off your guitar strings, I said, '*that's the one I've been looking for*.'"

"I know." Grace swallowed again. They *were* going to throw up, there wasn't a question about it. They just hoped that it would wait until after the show was over.

"I've been meaning to ask about how you wrote it." Bee kept going. Grace's head snapped up.

"What do you mean by that?" they asked sharply. Bee raised a dark eyebrow.

"The kind of things you must have been feeling, the experiences you were having. No one just pulls that kind of heartbreak out of nowhere. No one writes a song about getting manipulated, ruined, and abandoned unless they've been in the trenches of that sort of thing. So to speak."

"Oh." Grace forced themselves to take a deep breath. "Yeah, I was in a bad place with Amy."

Amy, with her long blond hair and her big doe eyes, lived rent-free in Grace's head for a baker's dozen of great and terrible reasons. Amy, who wrote beautiful music and had an angelic voice to go along with it. She really could have *been* somebody, if she wasn't such a bitch.

"If only she hadn't committed the ultimate sin of challenging you." Bee's voice was a little hazy in Grace's disoriented state. "It's a burden moving through such a delicate reality, where you can never be wrong. Or misperceived."

"What? Come again?" Grace brought themselves back to reality and looked over at Bee. He had finally taken off his sunglasses, and now he was staring at Grace with eyes that were so blue and bright they looked like bulbs on a Christmas tree.

"It's just an observation." Bee spread his hands.

"No, I mean, how can you know what I..." Grace was cut off by the audience's applause. They looked back towards the stage to see the emcee take over the mic while Penny broke down her set.

Bee brought his hand down to land against Grace's shoulder and he gave it a squeeze. "Good luck out there," he said. "I know they're going to love her song."

"It's my song," Grace said, without really thinking about it.

"Right," Bee said. "But it's about her, isn't it?"

Grace nodded. They didn't tear their eyes away from the stage. Suddenly, their knees were weak and there was a gallon of acid sloshing around in their stomach. They did not want to go on stage, they did not want to perform their set. They didn't want to go to Knoxville, either. They just wanted to run home, crawl under their covers, and cry themselves to sleep.

"You know," Bee said conversationally, "I had the pleasure of meeting Amy, myself. She's a lovely gal, and I can see why you were in love with her."

Grace looked at him, mortified, but he went on. "She told me that she wanted you to choke on her words. And I thought that was such an interesting choice of phrase. *Her* words, not *yours.* People say strange things when they're hurt, don't you suppose?"

"How did you meet Amy?" Grace didn't want to have this conversation now, not when they were about to go on stage, but they couldn't help themselves. "And *when?* I've known you since..."

"They're calling you up, we'll talk about it later." Bee winked and pulled out a cigar. He struck a match that cast its light briefly onto a 'no smoking backstage' sign.

"Later," Grace echoed. Nothing felt real, anymore. Here Bee was, telling them that he had met their ex—their *terrible, lying* ex. What had Amy told him? What *lies* about Grace was she spreading? If this cost them *anything,* Grace was going to freak out. If Bee dropped them as a client, if anyone even thought to accuse Grace of stealing their lyrics...

'Devil Caught My Roses' was a different matter, but it was the *only* one Grace had not one hundred percent written by themselves. But they had a *hand* in most of it, so it pretty much counted as their own work. They had inspired Amy to write the song and they had helped her workshop it until it sounded perfect. It wasn't Grace's fault that they had been the one to record it, first. And after everything, anyway, it was the *least* of what they were owed. Amy wouldn't understand that, she would just continue to spread lies. And people were going to believe her, because someone *always* did.

Grace transferred from the stool backstage to the stool onstage. This time, they held their electric guitar, plugged into its amp, and when they looked out towards the crowd all they saw were a few dozen dark shadows. The stage lights blocked out faces until they no longer seemed like real people. Grace's fingers started sweated, and they wiped their hands off on their pants before positioning their hands to play.

Their stomach trembled. Their lips parted. They didn't get past the first line.

Grace's stomach surged and sent a geyser of acid rocketing up their throat. Grace leaned over their guitar and spewed onto the stage, their whole body shaking violently as they gave up everything they had eaten in the past day and a half.

When they raised their head and looked out towards the crowd, the faceless shadows were silent. They waited for the emcee to come smooth things over while someone cleaned up the vomit, or for someone to at least *say* something. No one did.

Grace looked over towards the left stage wing, but all they saw was Bee standing there, puffing on his cigar.

They licked their lips and tried again. The handwritten lyrics were clipped to a music stand in front of them, and they tried to find their place even as Amy's squiggly handwriting began to swim around their vision.

Grace blinked and rubbed their eyes, still burning from the violent retching. They reached out to take the lyric sheet and pull it closer, hoping that would help.

They still couldn't read it. Amy's handwriting looked like it was sliding off the page. Grace didn't know what to do, the only possible solution was to—

--*eat it.* The intrusive thought stuck to the side of their brain, and it was all they could hear. *Eat it. Put the words inside of you.*

Grace pressed the lyric sheet against their tongue. The paper tasted slightly acidic, like a lemon. They used three fingers to keep going, pushing the paper into their mouth and back towards their throat. The sharp, crinkled ridges sliced their raw cheeks and tongue and made them sting. They kept shoving it back until it hit their uvula and then they retched again. Their hand deep in their mouth, halfway to their wrist, and they couldn't stop themselves from driving it deeper.

Suddenly, they couldn't breathe. They couldn't pull in a breath through their nose deeply enough to try and launch the paper out. It was lodged in their throat, and they choked, their face already hot and tingling.

Grace dropped their guitar and clutched their throat. They fell to the stage and landed on their side. Pain went singing up to their shoulder, but they couldn't even cry out. Their face was getting hotter while the rest of their body was ice cold, and they still couldn't breathe. No matter how much they gagged and wheezed, the paper would not dislodge.

Finally, for a whole minute, the world was quiet except for ringing in their ears. Grace found themselves staring up at the ceiling, right into the brightest stage light. They closed their eyes, hoping the darkness would just stay and end their misery.

When they opened their eyes again, they were back to sitting on their stool, guitar in their hands while facing a crowd of faceless shadows. Except this time, they had a gut-feeling that not one of the people in the crowd was real.

Their eyes fell to the music stand in front of them. The lyrics for 'Devil Caught My Roses' were clipped onto the front. Amy's handwriting was a lot sharper, now that their vision had cleared, although the paper was somehow damp around the corners.

Grace started to tremble.

"Try it again," Bee said from his place in the wings. "It'll go differently this time, I'm sure of it."

"I don't want to," Grace's voice broke. "I don't want to do this anymore."

"Sorry, kiddo, but it's tough shit. I've already reserved this spot for you, and it's all yours for a good long while." Smoke tickled their nose. "I'm heading out because I've got better things to do, but I think you'll like it here. All those faces. A captive audience. And not one of them is going to have a sideways thought about you. Mostly because none of them can have a single thought, at all." His grin was vicious. "Isn't that what you wanted?"

"No!" Grace's fingers slid over their guitar strings, even though they had no desire to try and sing again. They ground their teeth even as their stomach flipped again just like it had before. "What did Amy *tell you?*"

"Good luck, kiddo," the devil didn't answer them. "Hate to leave you in limbo, but you're making me queasy."

If he said anything else, Grace wasn't able to hear it. The first line of the song scraped its way through their clenched teeth, and another surge of vomit came tearing out of their throat with a scream.

There is a cowboy at the roulette table who has no face. Under the warm yellow lamp that swings over the table, blood and muscle glisten like red depression glass. He never speaks, but he loses every time the wheel spins. There is a rodeo show poster stuck to the back of his fringed jacket, but all the details underneath a drawing of his face have been rubbed away, including his name.

SUTTON

at the end of his rope

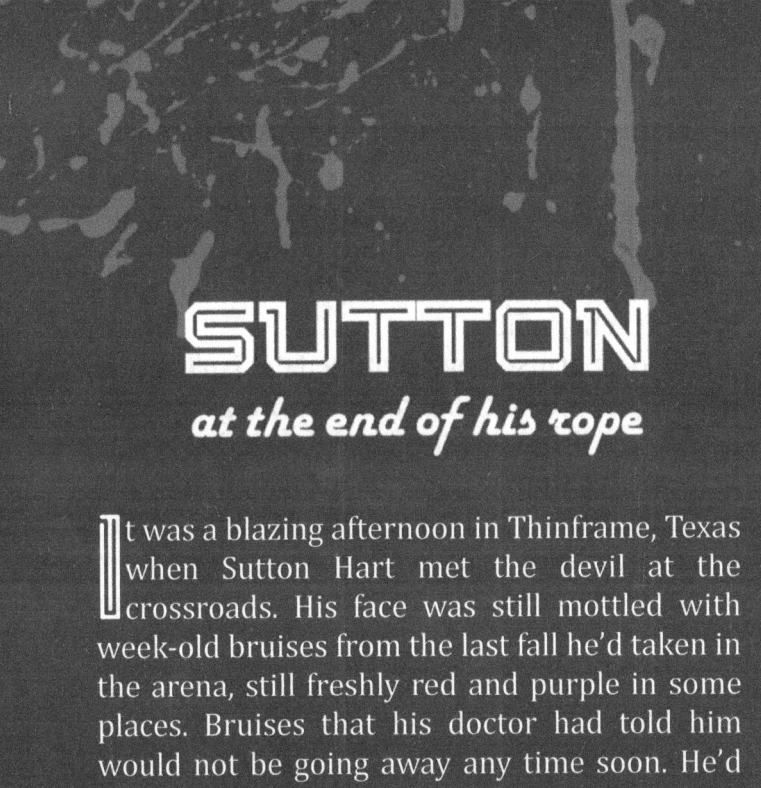

It was a blazing afternoon in Thinframe, Texas when Sutton Hart met the devil at the crossroads. His face was still mottled with week-old bruises from the last fall he'd taken in the arena, still freshly red and purple in some places. Bruises that his doctor had told him would not be going away any time soon. He'd been lucky to come out of that incident with no broken bones. For a rodeo cowboy past the age of 53, broken bones were a career death sentence, if not a literal one.

The shade cast from his hat brim kept the worst of it concealed. He had one cigarette left and he rolled it between his calloused fingers, taking his time to savor the experience. Smoke tickled the back of his throat and the robust tobacco made his tongue burn. He kept his eyes on the man in front of him, the devil who'd appeared in a white suit with combed black hair, flicking his tongue faster than an auctioneer.

"Is this the famous Sutton Hart who wants to make a deal with me?" the devil asked, as if Sutton had a reputation far preceding that of Ol' Mx. Slick. "I must admit, I didn't think that you were one I'd get. Pride isn't my bailiwick despite having plenty of it."

Sutton's bruised eye twitched. "It isn't pride, what I'm here for," he said. "Nothing prideful about crawling on your belly through the dust."

"I would know." The devil flashed a sharp grin. "So, what can I do you for, Mr. Hart? Your watch has been ticking for a while now. Your posters have become more faded than your blue jeans."

Sutton shifted his jaw and took another drag from his cigarette to avoid spitting in the dirt. *'Don't disrespect the devil on his own stomping grounds'*, was how his nana used to warn him.

Back then, it was to keep him from ripping bluebonnets up by the root along the dirt path behind her house, but now it wouldn't leave his head.

"I don't want to go out with a whimper," Sutton answered at last. "That's all. I'm not trying to do the impossible or anything, I know I can't go back in time and relive the glory days. And times have changed enough that there's no reviving them in the same way, either. But Lord—I'm sorry if that offends you—I want to stay strong until the end. My career. My body. Everything, for as long as I have left. I want them screaming my name from the stands."

Hearing it come from his own mouth was disorienting. Because, yes, that was what he wanted. It was *exactly* what he wanted, but he'd never asked for it before. Never even thought to pray about it in church because it seemed wrong to ask God for more than he'd be given. At the very least, it was ungrateful. Sutton's desperation was born out of pure greed, he was convinced. Wanting more and more of what he'd already had, time and time again.

The devil smiled and pulled out a cigar of his own. He produced a black box out of nowhere and offered one to Sutton, who pitched his stubby cigarette into the dirt to accept.

"You're so close to self-awareness, and I think that's mighty fine coming from a man like you.

Men born in the thick of the Great Depression tend to be a little big for their britches, as if sawing grit between your teeth in the Dust Bowl was some kind of cosmic hazing that entitles you to greatness. Not you, Sutton."

"I earned my greatness," Sutton said. "Through every scrape and bruise. Hell, I lost a few teeth just to gain a little ground."

"You know the price?" the devil switched topics. Sutton could see his interest waning through his expression. "You know what I'm going to take from you?"

"I've got a hunch," Sutton said. "But whatever you could want, I likely don't have much use for these days."

"Of course, you'd think that." The devil set his teeth against the end of his cigar. "All right then, Mr. Hart. There's just one extra step I need you to take."

"What step is that?" The cigar smoke was heavier and thicker than the wispy, pitiful ribbons that had come from his cigarette. It filled his nose and throat and forced Sutton to clear his throat three times in succession.

"I'm going to need you get down on your hands and knees, and crawl," the devil grinned. "Just to make sure this *isn't* a matter of pride. You understand."

Sutton sucked on his teeth so hard he tasted blood. He balled his free hand up into a fist and pressed it to his side, trying to keep himself grounded enough to not lose his temper and, consequentially, his only opportunity. The old Sutton would have thrown up both middle fingers and told the devil to go fuck himself. But the old Sutton wouldn't be here, because he didn't *have* to be.

And he could sit there agonizing over it, or he could take a breath, close his eyes, and do it. Then it would all be over. Then he could get back to the corral, to his horse, and to his lasso.

Sutton dropped to his knees hard enough that his teeth rattled in his head. He threw himself forward and caught himself on his hands, which made his palms sting. Sutton looked up at the devil who smiled down at him with a single gold fang more glaring than the sun.

"Still feels like there's something miss," the devil said. "Oh, I know." He took a step back. "Crawl to me, on your belly."

Sutton exhaled hard enough that his nostrils flared. There was something purely bestial in what he was being made to do. All this, and without even a guarantee. But he had a feeling that questioning the devil was a lot like questioning God—if you planted that seed of doubt, then your lack of faith would work against you.

Sutton lowered himself until his stomach and chin were lined up on the ground. Then, slowly, he dragged himself across the dirt and towards the devil's gleaming white shoes. Every time he got close enough to touch them, the devil took another step back, and Sutton growled. He kept dragging himself along, dirt and dry grass scraping his belly as friction pushed his shirt up. It felt like an hour, then two hours, then it had to be pushing three, and he just kept crawling. The devil never told him to stop. Those white shoes were his only focus, although the sun made them unbearably bright.

Finally, the devil came to a stop, and Sutton collapsed to the ground. He pressed his face against the dirt for a minute and let himself lay there, purely dry-mouthed and exhausted.

"You okay there, Sutton?" The voice belonged to another roper, Nash, and not the devil who had led him here. Sutton's head came up and he craned his neck for a better look. Black boots, dirty blond hair, dingy checkered shirt. Yeah, that was Nash.

"Holy hell," he muttered. Sutton pushed himself up onto his knees and then slowly rose to his feet. He kept his arms out for balance, while Nash held out a hand, but Sutton didn't take it.

"I'm fine," Sutton said. "I was just stretching out my back."

Nash raised a blond eyebrow but didn't question him. "We're starting in about half an hour and I figured you'd want to get into your Western wear." He held out a half-drained water bottle and Sutton accepted it with a nod, twisting off the top and chugging the contents.

He drank the rest of the bottle, and it still didn't slake his thirst. His mouth was drier than ever.

"You sure you're all right?" Nash asked. Behind them, the speakers blared an announcement of the upcoming lineup. When they heard the name Sutton Hart, the entire stadium erupted into cheers.

Sutton grinned and wiped the dirt off his chin, crumpling up the water bottle in his fists.

"I'm doing great," he said. "Come on, let's hop to it."

Nash turned around and led the way. Sutton followed him, and as they passed through the gate, though he caught a glimpse of gleaming white cowboy boots.

His heart skipped a beat and his head snapped up, but there was nothing in his line of vision except a grey steer.

The devil had followed Sutton Hart all the way from the dusty crossroads to the Black Buzzard Arena, but he did not realize it until the very last moment. It was easy to ignore the prickling on the back of his neck, mistaking it for sweat. His nerves before a good rodeo show always made his stomach feel tight, so there was no reason to believe that his roiling gut might have been trying to pull his attention towards something else.

From the shower to the gate, Sutton had tried to push the devil to the back of his mind. The details of the afternoon's encounter already starting to fade. Everything was on its way to becoming a blur of bruised purple clouds against an orange popsicle sky. He hacked up the tickle that remained from the smoldering cigar smoke and dampened it with chew he'd gotten from Nash and shoved down into his cheek. He blotted out the memory of those cold blue eyes, shielded by purple lenses, to focused on the present.

He had a steer to rope. And even though his heels burned inside his boots and the prickling on his neck was painful, like it was swollen from a wasp sting, he could not turn and run away. He could not disappoint the crowd. Not when they finally wanted him again.

Sutton spat out his chew and grabbed his cowboy hat from its peg on the wall. His anxiety was relieved, just a little, by the thunderous applause coming again from the stands. Maybe the crowd hadn't come for him specifically, but they *were* cheering for him all the same. Maybe now, his face on a flyer would go back to meaning something. Maybe those stands would *stay* full.

Let the shareholders take *that* to the bank. It could have been all the devil's doing, but he was not going to sit there and wonder.

His quarter-horse was waiting for him, a beautiful palomino appropriately named Sonny. They had done a lot of work together, and Sutton patted that cream-colored neck as he mounted. It was the calm before the storm, getting his stirrups and his rope checked before all hell broke loose. The chaos of the arena was what he loved. It was the adrenaline that made his heart pound until he felt like it was going to burst.

It all came down to the work of a few seconds. In the end it was him, his partner, and the steer.

He had done it a million times. When they opened the gate, he dug his heels into the horse's flanks.

For half a second, he was blinded by the arena lights. Being astride a quarter-horse tearing through the dirt at a break-neck pace was a lot like flying, or as close to flying as he could get without being thrown off a bull's back. The white steer with its wide, dark-tipped horns ran beside him and Sutton urged his horse closer, pulling Sonny in so that the steer had nowhere to go while the dark horse of his heeler closed in on the flank.

Sutton grabbed his rope. He swung it up into the air and glanced over at the heeler to give a brief signal. The other rider looked back at him, and for a moment, Sutton was trapped in a flash of blue. It washed over his vision and he ground his teeth, unable to stop himself from throwing his arm over his face to try and block it out. The acrid smell of cigar smoke filled his nose and pricked the back of his throat, and he gagged. He dropped his rope trying to regain his composure and went to grip his saddle horn, but his gloves slipped. He slid off the side of his saddle with one foot still caught in the stirrup, shouting and swearing as Sonny continued to drag him through the arena.

Sutton's head knocked against something hard and a loud, angry crack sounded off through the inside of his skull like a shot. His foot finally came loose from the stirrup and his leg thudded against the ground as he lay there, groaning and dazed, with the hot arena lights so bright above his head that he could not see the stands or the ceiling.

He could still hear the crowd, but barely. Their hoots and hollers had faded into a dull echo, sounding more like mockery than genuine enthusiasm. Their voices were drowned out by the sound of hard-soled boots striking the ground. Each step was crystal-clear like a hammer smashing granite, even over the ringing in his ears.

Finally, the steps came to a halt. There was a man standing next to him, and when he leaned over, Sutton caught a whiff of cigar smoke and Aqua Velva like a preacher's necktie on Sunday. The man raised one boot into the air and rested it against Sutton's chest, grinding the heel down right on his sternum—only just lightly enough to let him breathe.

"Sutton Hart." He had the devil's blue eyes hidden behind a pair of round purple sunglasses, and when he smiled he flashed a vicious gold canine that was just a little bit sharper than the rest. Sutton's next breath forced his chest to press against the white boot that was bearing down on it. His attempt to speak came out more as a whimper, and he could barely hear himself over the roaring crowd and blood rushing through his ears.

"What are they saying?" he asked. He hated the way his own voice sounded, thin and weak.

"Your adoring masses?" The devil cupped his hand around his ear. "They are chanting your name, cowboy. Can't you hear it?"

"I just…" Sutton swallowed. His whole mouth tasted like blood, and he choked a bit. "I don't want the deal. I made a mistake."

"I figured that." The devil pulled a thick cigar out from his white fringe jacket, already lit, and placed it between his teeth. "You crawled away before our business was concluded. But you see, I do something for you, you do something for me. That's how it works. No amount of blubbering is going to get you out of that."

Gray ash dribbled from the end of his cigar and landed in Sutton's eye. Hot tears welled up to flush it out. He tried to raise his hand to wipe it away, but his arm would not move. He tried not to panic.

"You haven't done anything for me," Sutton gasped. The devil was just a blur in front of him, now. White leather and slicked-back hair darker than a crow's feather. It all blended together until the only standout shape was the bright orange circle of his burning cigar.

"That is where you are wrong," the devil said. He ground his boot down a little harder, and something in Sutton's chest crackled. "You wanted to feel famous again. Well, Mr. Hart. I made you famous for life. I can *guarantee* that no one in this arena will ever forget your name." He drew every word out lazily on his tongue, as if he had all day. Sutton shivered underneath his boot. A deep, painful chill had started to settle into his bones—like it had been resting on his skin and was now sinking all the way down to the marrow.

"What do you mean?" Sutton gasped.

"First man to die in Black Buzzard Arena in what, fifty years?" The devil laughed. "What's not to talk about?"

Panic gripped his heart and sent fear like ice water snaking through his veins. Sutton cried out in agony and tried to bite the sound back with his teeth.

"I am not dead!" Sutton tried to sit up, but he could not lift his head. He might as well have been nailed down.

"Not yet," the devil said. The laughter had been chased out of his voice, and now his words were as cold as steel.

"What do you want, then?" Sutton racked his brain for the answer even as the question stumbled from his lips.

"I told you at the crossroads," the devil teased. "Don't you remember? Or were you too busy chewing on the dust and taking off? Are you starting to think my price is too high?" The devil finally moved his boot from Sutton's chest, although that did not make it any easier to breathe. He swayed his hips and swung his leg over the fallen cowboy's body, lowering himself down until he was straddling Sutton's shoulders. The devil took another long drag from his cigar and leaned over, placing his lips close to Sutton's ear and pushing the words out on a thick cloud of dark gray smoke. "You could have asked, and I would have been honest about it. I value honesty, you know. I would have told you that at the end of your life, you would be mine. Husk, heart, and soul. I could peel back your skin like a rind and eat your heart like the jeweled flesh of an orange...oh, is that not what you had in mind?"

Suddenly, it was too hard to swallow. Sutton felt all his words bubbling up on a geyser of spittle that would not go down. And he was cold, so very cold. Even if he could move, he was not certain that he could get very far before his bones snapped.

"I know it is hard, getting old," the devil said. "You want to be the face that everyone loves and admires for decades to come. But you've been around the arena, cowboy, more than a few times. Someone else is always going to be waiting in line to take your place. You wanted it enough to ask for it, but not enough to see it through. And if there is one thing I cannot abide..." the devil slid his purple glasses down the stern bridge of his nose, "it is a coward."

"P-please," Sutton began to stammer. He spat up enough that it started to run down the sides of his bearded cheek. "It doesn't...I am sorry."

"Shh." The devil spoke to him like he was a child. He cradled Sutton's head with cool, pale hands and stroked his temples. Those blue eyes consumed Sutton's vision until he was lost in their deep, infinite pools. The pupils at their center widened, spreading fast like drops of ink on rain-soaked newspaper. They reached out towards the dark rims and the blue folded over him like a blanket, except it was not warm. The devil's world was cold and still, like being dead, although he was still completely aware.

He could feel things. He could *hear* things. Yet he could no longer move.

Something pricked his temple, like the devil was digging his nails into the skin until it broke with a soft *'pop'*. Sutton's skin stung as it was peeled back, his flesh coming up with it in long, burning strips.

Now he was warm, again. Hot blood poured from the wound and pooled underneath his head. It soaked through his shirt and stuck to his chest as the devil went back up for more. Another long strip came away, and this time the devil held it up in front of his eyes, wiggling it back and forth like a banner.

"I could have been a bullfighter," the devil laughed. He opened his mouth and let the ribbon of flesh pile lazily onto his unnaturally long, red tongue. He placed his nail against Sutton's temple again, peeling back another long strip, while the cowboy jerked involuntarily underneath him. There was more flesh than skin in the devil's hands this time, and he pulled it apart like a soft plum, placing bits and pieces on his tongue and pushing it around his mouth to savor every last bit of the taste before swallowing.

"Not quite like steer," he said, "but nothing beats the taste of cowboy." He leaned over again, placing his hands on either side of Sutton's head as he drew his tongue up from the man's jaw to his earlobe. "It did not have to end this way, you know. But if you are worried about the crowd, I can assure you that they do not know the difference. Once I have taken my due entirely, they will have a mercifully different visual. What do you think would be more fitting? Being crushed underneath a steer's hooves, or having your ribs broken under your fallen horse?"

Even if there had been an answer, Sutton could not summon it. The pain in his head pulsed through his entire body, making every muscle twitch in agony. There was nothing he could do. He could not even close his eyes to shut out the sight of the devil's blood-stained teeth and his long tongue, or those bluebonnet eyes that made him feel as though the whole world had gone still.

Finally, the devil pulled back. Despite the blood on his teeth and chin, there was nothing on his spotless white fringe jacket. He put his cigar back between his teeth, somehow still smoldering, and stood up. His hard-soled boots hit the ground with all the fervor of a judge's gavel.

"It was nice doing business with you," he said, and he winked. A shiver ran up Sutton's body, and it coiled in his stomach like a physical punch to the gut. He could not even feel the pain in his temple any longer, all he knew was hate.

The devil walked away, disappearing into the multicolored arena lights. The sound of the crowd climbed, growing even louder until it drowned out everything else.

And then all his senses came back at once. He was back on the horse and he could smell its sweat mingling with the bull dung from the pens. He could taste the dirt that was being flung up into his face, gritty between his teeth. The crowd was chanting his name, and he could breathe. He could see every muscle rippling beneath the steer's gleaming white coat as it charged between him and the heeler.

His heeler. *The devil.*

Fear pulled Sutton's head up, and the fraction of lost concentration cost him. The horse flanking the steer was not pitch black like it had been before, but brown, although it did not matter now. The steer charged and Sonny balked. The palomino flung him from his back, and Sutton went sailing through the air. The crowd inhaled sharply, and someone screamed when he hit the ground. The impact sent a shiver through his body, and the crackle from his ribcage filled his ears.

Sutton pushed himself up on his elbow and flung himself onto his back. His vision was lost to the arena lights once again, but the devil's words would not leave his head.

'First man to die in Black Buzzard's Arena in what, fifty years?'

It was not the fame he had sought after. But then, he supposed that was something of his fault. He should have been more specific.

'Devil in the details.' Was his next thought. For some reason, that made him laugh. The sound came scraped out from his broken chest and flew out on a mouthful of blood.

His mouth was still open when the galloping steer's hoof came down on his face.

There is a woman who hovers near one of the poker tables, and she's dressed like an Old Hollywood starlet. Her gown is deep crimson, her hair is platinum blond, and she leaves ruby lipstick prints on the end of a silver cigarette holder. From the shoulders-up, she is a vision. However, underneath the gown, as all the residents will tell you, she is nothing but a water-logged skeleton dripping with vegetation and clogged with mud. She is more than willing to talk to you about her illustrious film career, but if she tries to talk about her death, she will start coughing up water and no longer be able to speak.

RUBY
the next best thing since apple pie

uby Suede was going to be famous, and her face was going to be on life-size posters like the ones hanging on the powder-blue diner walls. She was going to be the second most recognizable person on a TV screen—second only because she wouldn't dream of outshining The Duke, the head-to-toe rhinestoned country singer who inspired her to change her name. *Suede* rolled off the tongue so much easier than *Swayze*. And Ruby wanted her name to be easy to scream and shout, over and over again.

She daydreamed about it while staring at the faded, water-stained poster of Duke Blakely that hung right next to the entrance door. Her only complaint was that it was also right across from the cash register, which meant that sometimes a customer's head would get in the way.

By 2:30AM, her shift was not an exciting one. The truckers who trickled in off the highway were more exhausted than chatty and all they were really interested in was something hot to eat before catching a few hours' sleep. Ruby slid coffee mugs and pie-bearing plates across the counter and tore tickets off her pad all in relative silence. The only background noise was from the old black-and-white TV mounted in the far corner, and she kept it turned down because it mostly played sermons.

By the time the devil walked in, the place was empty, and the sound of her own voice caught her off guard.

"Welcome in, have a seat anywhere." Ruby paced down the length of the counter to grab a menu and slid it his way. He just looked like a man, with nothing really 'off' except for the fact that it was pitch-black outside and he was wearing sunglasses. He sat down at the counter and immediately pulled out a cigar, making himself comfortable without even looking at the menu.

Ruby crinkled her nose.

"What can I get ya?" she asked, if for no other reason than to have an excuse to walk away.

"I see you have apple pie, I'll take that. Do you mind the smoke?" The devil flashed a grin.

"All the truckers who come through here smoke," Ruby said, stepping aside to grab a slice of pie from its clear glass case. "I just don't like to breathe it. I'm trying to preserve my voice."

"What for?" he asked as she set the plate in front of him.

"I'm going to be an actress." Ruby smiled for the first time in hours. Her cheeks felt a little sore as they stretched. "I want to be one of those girls who acts and sings, like Barbara Streisand."

"You've got the face for it," the devil said. He picked up his fork and sank the prongs through the pie's top crust. "But you know, talent discoveries aren't made in diners."

Ruby's smile fell and she hugged her chest. "You never know," she said, trying to maintain her pleasant waitress tone. "All kinds of people come through here."

"You have a point, but I have one too. This is rural Tennessee. Darlin', I don't mean to burst your bubble, but there's miles of mountains between you and the nearest California talent scout. The only reason a big-shot Hollywood executive would be blowing his way through here would be if he got lost on his way to a cruise down in Florida."

Ruby set her jaw. "Can I get you anything else?" she asked, with her tone a lot shorter this time around.

"Coffee would be nice." The devil took a puff off his cigar. "Don't look so glum. There's still hope."

"How do you figure?" Ruby turned around and grabbed the coffee pot from its burner. It was a shame that she couldn't let some 'accidentally' pour all over his lap. It'd definitely stain that spotless white suit.

"Do you gamble?"

Ruby's back straightened and she filled an off-white coffee cup almost to its brim.

"No," she said. "My daddy lost a lot of money playing poker."

"I'm not talking about poker, I'm talking about blackjack." From out of nowhere, the devil produced a deck of sleek black cards and set them on the diner counter. "Do you know how to play?"

"Yes." Ruby eyed the cards. Her stomach tightened just looking at them. "But what are we playing for?"

The devil gripped his cigar between his teeth and held up one finger. He reached into his suit blazer and pulled out a wad of cash—more bills squeezed together by a rubber band than Ruby had ever seen in her life. He set the cash down on the counter and her heart started beating so fast that she thought she was going to throw up.

"Twenty thousand dollars," the devil said. "Tomorrow's New Year's, isn't it?"

Ruby nodded. She didn't tear her eyes away from the money.

"That money will get you to California and set you up nice and pretty while you're looking for that talent agent."

"Why would you give it to me?" *Fear*, she realized. That was the feeling sitting at the bottom of her stomach that was making her palms sweat.

"I'm not giving you anything, sweetheart, you'll be playing for it." The devil cut his fork through the pie again. "Money isn't everything, and I sure as hell don't need it."

Ruby leaned forward, feeling a little dazed. No part of this exchange felt real, but the money was there, and *it* was real. She wanted to hold it in her hands, just to know what it was like. Twenty grand was *almost* what Duke Blakely had spent on his mansion. She could get out to

California, get an apartment of her own, maybe some voice lessons...

"What do you get if I lose?" she finally brought herself around to ask. The devil's grin sharpened.

"You assume that I want you to lose, or that I would let you. A game can be rigged both ways," he said.

"Then why not just give it to me?" Ruby swallowed down a lump.

"Because there's no sport in that, darlin'. But let's say you lose. All right, you still get twenty grand, but I'll go with you to California."

Ruby's breath got stuck and she choked.

"What do you mean, you'll go with me?" she asked faintly.

"Exactly what it sounds like. I know my way around Hollywood, honey, believe me. I can introduce you to all the right people who can get you in all the right pictures." He leaned forward, propping his elbow up on the counter. "And what do I get out of that? Well, frankly, I know what Hollywood does to a perfectly fine soul. Starlets are like diamonds, and I mean that they go through enormous, crushing amounts of pressure to form. You're a little piece of coal right now, but they can polish you up, and then what's left of your soul will be nothing but gunk. But that gunk is what some might call a *delicacy* to someone like me."

He'd stopped making sense. Once he started about her soul, Ruby lost all understanding of the conversation. She watched his tan fingers drum against the countertop, gold rings flashing across every knuckle. No matter how many times she blinked and tried to clear her head, the deck of cards was still there, and so was the money.

What, realistically, did she have to lose?

"All right," Ruby said. "I'll play."

The devil stuck his cigar back inside his broad grin and picked up the cards to shuffle. They were black on both sides, the suits only marked by spot-shined designs and numbers.

"That's the kind of brass I like," the devil said. "And just think, you're set either way."

"Why don't you want me to lose?" Ruby leaned against the counter and watched the cards being shuffled, as if she had any eye for chicanery. In truth, he could be sticking them up his sleeve and she wouldn't be able to tell.

"Maybe I have an inkling about the woman you could become," he said. "Maybe I can see into your future."

Ruby rolled her eyes. "I think you're just a guy who likes blondes," she countered. "And you're being really, *really* strange about it."

"I'll tell you right now, darlin', blondes aren't my type by a long-shot," the devil said. "But what I *can* appreciate is a woman with a stinger.

You're about as All-American as a Fourth of July Playboy spread, they'll eat you up and you'll ride that as far as you can. And you'll take it *far*. You've got poison in you that you've not even thought to tap into yet." The devil slapped a few cards onto the counter and then looked up expectantly.

"Hit me," Ruby said. Another card came down. "Hit me." She barely looked, she just kept her eyes on the devil.

Another card slapped against the cracked linoleum. "Busted," the devil's blue eyes sparked behind his purple lenses. "Do you want another shot, or are you content to let me tag along?"

"What does a second chance cost me?" Ruby asked.

"You're so clever. You know nothing is ever free." The devil paused while he set his cigar down on his plate and sipped his coffee. "If you lose again, I take ten grand away."

It was like being hit in the chest with a mallet. Ruby took a step back. "That's a bastard move," she said.

"It's no fun otherwise." The devil was already re-shuffling the cards. "Silver screen or Tennessee pines. Up to you, honey."

Ten grand wasn't bad. Ten grand was a *hell* of a lot more than she had now. But it wasn't going to get her as far. Twenty would carry her through the whole year if she was smart.

Besides, if he was telling the truth, then there were a whole lot of people she could skip the line to meet. She wouldn't *need* to budget for a year on her own. It could be six months, or less. She'd be an overnight sensation and she'd be starring in pictures by Christmas. If he was lying...

'If he's lying, we'll be crossing an awful lot of state lines.' The thought popped into her head as a voice that wasn't her own. It made her jump and she squeaked her fingertips over the countertop.

The devil laughed. "Are you thinking about killing me already?" He started laying the cards out. "*Stinger*, I told you, that's what I like."

"I'm not..." Ruby trailed off and shook her head. She waited for a beat to chase the unwanted thought out. "I'm not thinking about...no." She set her hand down on top of the black cards. "I'll ride with you to California," she said. "I'm not giving up ten grand and cutting my chances in half."

"It's not death row, darlin', you don't need to look so grim about it," the devil said. "And my company's not as bad as all that."

She wasn't so sure, but she wasn't going to voice that doubt, either. Ruby extended her hand. "I want to hang onto it myself," she said. "That's *my* condition."

He looked her up and down, then he picked up the cash and handed it over without a fuss. "Fine by me, love, don't spend it all on bubblegum and records. Once you're out, you're out."

Ruby rolled her eyes and stuffed the cash down into her skirt pocket. The wad was so thick that it barely fit. "I don't get off until 5," she muttered.

"Why wait?" he asked.

"I need to get my things, then." She just needed a *minute* away from this man. Ruby pulled on her apron strings and vanished into the back. She hadn't realized just how *directly* she could feel his eyes burning into her until she was out of his sight.

With her apron hanging loose around her neck, Ruby sat down in a chair and buried her face in her hands. She wanted to cry, but she didn't have time for that. So much was changing at once, and she had to make quick decisions, or she was going to lose every opportunity she had just been handed. Quite literally, *handed over.*

'*Why wait?*' the devil had asked her. Ruby raised her head and looked at the back door.

Why wait? She didn't need to go with anyone. She had a car. She knew these backroads and could drive them in her sleep. Let him try to find her where the pines grew thicker than tar and there were miles of mountainside road without guardrails.

She didn't even give herself a chance to think twice. Ruby pulled off her apron and snagged her purse from its hook before grabbing the back door by its steel handle. The door resisted at first, and her heart plummeted into her gut, but then she gave the handle another yank and the door swung open.

Muggy air hit her in the face, but Ruby didn't dare pause. She started running for her car. The only thing louder than the screaming cicadas was the blood roaring through her ears. Her car was a beater passed down from her older brother, and the tires were balder than a church deacon, but in her mind that just meant she could go *fast*.

The engine turned over and Ruby began praying. She peeled out of the parking lot and sped right past the diner, and only then did she spare it a glance.

The sign's light was off and all the windows were dark. The door had its big chain wrapped around the bar and the place looked like it had been abandoned for months. Ruby furrowed her brow, confused, and had to swerve to avoid hitting the sign pole at the entrance.

Her back tires fishtailed and she fought to regain control. The wad of cash had found its way underneath her rear and it was like sitting on a stone.

Ruby barely avoided cruising sideways onto the highway. When she finally got her car to stop, she looked back towards the diner, just to make sure she wasn't imagining things.

It was still dark. The only difference was that the devil stood in the doorway, smoking his cigar and watching her. All Ruby could see of his eyes was the reflection of orange sparks in his purple lenses.

The devil raised his hand like he was waving. Ruby gripped her steering wheel and floored it.

Maybe he wasn't in a hurry, but that didn't mean he wouldn't come after her. She had to get as far away as she could, as quickly as possible.

She would drive all the way to California as if the flames of hell were licking at her heels.

Hell's Belles has a private room where you can only enter if you're not meant to stay. Inside it's a vision of a cozy living room that makes you nostalgic for your own childhood home. There are framed pictures everywhere of the same woman in various stages of her life, and the floral couch has a white crocheted shawl draped over the back. Near an old radio, a single black candle burns. The radio plays the same song all day, no matter how long you sit there; 'Dedicated to the One I Love'.

OLIVIA

one last dance

It was supposed to be her fortieth wedding anniversary, but the only flowers she received were from the funeral home. Attached to the vase was a little white card with a perfunctory *'our thoughts are with you'* printed on one side. The flowers were beautiful, if a little droopy— but then again, she had always liked Easter Lilies. Harold would have brought her daisies from the grocery store along with two moon pies and a Coca-Cola for them to split. She would have said something like, "you forgot the peanuts," and he would have grinned as he said, "aren't I nuts enough for you, Liv?"

God, she missed him. There was a couple at their church celebrating sixty years and going strong next weekend. Both were in their eighties, while Harold had collapsed and died just shy of sixty-five.

Some things just weren't fair.

Her stomach hurt. Olivia stretched out on her couch with her dead husband's sweater bunched up underneath her head as a pillow. It still smelled like him: tobacco and laundry detergent. She tried not to wonder how long it would take for the scent to fade. For the last bits of Harold to slip out of her life, just like he had slowly slipped away the week he was sent home from the hospital.

The digital clock resting on top of the living room TV let her know that it was damn near midnight, and that she ought to go to bed. Unfortunately, she couldn't even bring herself to lift her head. There was just no point, in any of it, at all.

A knock on her apartment door startled her enough that it kicked her heart into overdrive. Olivia sat up so quickly that her vision swam and she nearly fell over. There was no reason for anyone to be on her doorstep at such an indecent hour, and she could only guess that it was one of those druggie college kids next door who might have wandered out, and now they were trying to get back through the wrong way. Olivia stayed quiet, hoping they would go away, but the knock only came again.

Olivia pursed her lips and got off the couch. She walked over to the door, hugging her chest as she leaned forward to peer through the peephole. It was too dark to see anything on the other side. She muttered a quick prayer before unlocking her door and pulling it open, but only as far as the chain above her head would allow.

The dim living room light escaped from over her shoulder and slipped through the narrow opening to illuminate the figure of a man. He wasn't much taller than she was, but he was handsome and tan, with purple sunglasses like he had just stepped off a cruise to Cabo. He was also absolutely young enough to be her son.

"You have the wrong apartment," she said before he had a chance to speak.

"I don't think so, Liv," he told her. The nickname caused her stomach to drop and sent a spike of fear up the length of her spine. Liv swallowed hard and took a step back, gripping her doorknob with the intent to slam the door shut. The man standing in the dark slid his hand onto the doorframe, in what Liv considered to be a bold show of confidence that she wouldn't just slam it *anyway* on his fingers.

"You don't need to be so worried," he said with a smile. "You asked for me."

"Did I?" She didn't budge an inch.

"*Anything for one more night.*" He spoke like he was quoting her directly and then puffed on a reeking cigar. The tobacco smell was familiar enough to be comforting, and Liv gripped the doorknob so hard she was sure she would leave a dent.

"I don't know what you're talking about," she said. She blamed the smoke for making her tear up. "But like I said, you have the wrong apartment. Now...get out of here." Her voice faltered. She couldn't even finish with something like *'or I'll call the cops'.*

"I can explain it from here, or from in there." The man on the other side shrugged. "Either way, I think you have a feeling in your gut." He looked her up and down with eyes so shockingly blue they were visible from behind his purple lenses. "I'm the one who comes when you're at your most desperate hour. And I'm not here to hurt you."

Most desperate? She wasn't so sure about that. Liv could think of a dozen times when she had felt more desperate than this. When she and Harold had nearly lost their house. When their daughter had to get her appendix taken out and they didn't know if insurance was going to cover the surgery. When Harold was in the hospital and the doctor said there was nothing more they could do, other than keep him comfortable.

"But you weren't alone then, were you?" the man asked, even though she hadn't spoken any of those thoughts aloud. "And you're alone now."

Olivia's hands trembled. She was a religious woman, but she had always been skeptical when someone gave a testimony about running into an angel at a grocery store, or hearing God's voice while they were driving. Now, she wished she had paid more attention. When an angel paid for your groceries, did you feel like your knees were going to buckle underneath you? When you heard God's voice telling you to take a different exit than usual, and then you narrowly avoid a horrible traffic accident, did you want to start crying because you felt like the weight of the world was being lifted from your shoulders?

Did angels make you feel like you were being weighed and measured by your worth, and did you feel like you were caught in the path of an apex predator when you watched them dart their tongue across their teeth?

The man slid his fingers back and Olivia closed the door. She could have left it there, she realized, but she didn't think it would end there if she did. She swept the chain back and then opened the door all the way. Olivia stepped back and gestured for the man to come in without saying a word.

"Much obliged." The man slid his hands into his pockets and stepped over the threshold. Olivia crinkled her nose.

"Put your cigar out," she said. "I don't allow smoking in my home."

"Oh, of course." He seemed amused. He pinched the blazing end out between his fingers, which was alarming because the cherry was nearly as big as a coal, and the cigar vanished altogether when he pulled it from his mouth. He must have stuck it into the pocket of his flawlessly white suit. She didn't know why he would do that, but she didn't have another explanation for its disappearance, either.

"Can I make you some coffee?" she asked. She wasn't sure how to start the conversation, or even what she wanted to ask. In fact, the longer he stood there, the less sure she was of why she had allowed him in, in the first place.

"Coffee? It's your anniversary." He looked at her and smiled, flashing a single gold canine that was ostensibly sharp. "I think wine would be more appropriate."

Oliva scoffed softly. "I don't have any," she said, not questioning how he knew. Her hands still trembled. "I've been back and forth from the funeral home all week, actually. I don't have much, period."

"I might surprise you. May I?" He didn't even wait for a response. The strange man strolled towards her kitchen and then opened the refrigerator, bending to glance at the racks before reaching in and pulling out a wine bottle by its neck.

Oliva's heart started beating so fast that her whole chest hurt. "How-?"

The man bopped the refrigerator door shut with his hip and flipped the bottle over in his hands. "No label," he said. "My guess is blueberry wine. You and your husband shared a bottle on your wedding night, didn't you?" He turned around and flipped open one of her cabinet doors, reaching in and bringing out two glasses—as if he knew where everything was. As if he was perfectly at home.

"Something like that," Olivia said quietly, watching him.

"*Something* like that." The man uncorked the wine bottle and began pouring. "You drank more of it than he did. And then the two of you ate the rest of your wedding cake and you had *so much* sex. It was, what, seven in the morning before you even went to bed?"

Olivia squeezed her eyes shut and ground her palms against them. She couldn't stop the flow of tears any longer, and they burned. "Stop that," she was almost begging. "Stop, I don't want to think about it."

"I know it's still painful." The man picked up one of the glasses and swirled the wine around a bit, letting it breathe. "You're leaking sorrow everywhere. You smell like it." He extended the glass across the counter towards her. "Do you know the smell of grief?"

Olivia shook her head and accepted the glass.

"Burnt sugar," the man said. "Like leaving caramel on the stove too long."

Olivia didn't have anything to say to that. She drained half her glass and then pushed her fingers through the grey roots of her bottle blonde hair, looking around the room. "You said *'anything for one more night'*, but you're not Harold," she finally said.

"No, I'm not," he said. "You can call me Bee." He walked up to her, holding his own glass.

"I don't know what you are..." She still couldn't look at him. "And I don't want to know. But you can't bring him back, can you?"

"No," he said. "But I can give you one last, very fine anniversary." He reached out with his free hand and touched her waist. Olivia's heart was practically galloping.

"And then what?" she asked, her voice breaking.

"Nothing you'll feel, or see, or know," Bee's voice cradled the pumping organ in her chest, easing it to slow. "Come on now, mama, don't concern yourself with particulars."

Olivia drained the rest of her glass.

"Switch on that radio," she said, gesturing to the one sitting on her countertop. "I want to dance."

"My kind of gal." Bee did just that. He set his wine glass down and turned the blue radio on. *Dedicated To The One I Love* started playing, and Olivia's tears were like a broken faucet. They just kept running and she had no control over them anymore.

"Harold liked to sing this to me," she whispered, her words ending in a hiccup.

Bee moved close to her, sweeping up her hand in his big one while putting his arm around her waist.

He smelled like tobacco and clean laundry. His suit blazer was warm like he'd been out in the sun, and his purple sunglasses were now resting on top of his slicked-back, coal-black hair. His blue eyes held her, rendering her breathless, while the weight of her grief and pain melted down into her toes before disappearing altogether.

"It's a beautiful song," he crooned. "A beautiful night." He leaned in closer and pressed his lips against her ear, humming along with the words before singing the chorus in a rich, deep Southern accent that reminded her of childhood, of warm summer nights spent picking brown pecans off the hood of her father's truck.

They danced in the space where the living room joined with the kitchen, swaying from carpet to tile while the song played. Olivia could have stayed in that place forever, with her head resting against this man's chest and her eyes closed, thinking about Harold, thinking about their wedding.

When the song ended, the radio faded out to a crackle. If Bee was controlling it somehow, he wasn't going to let the moment transition into something else. Bee's fingers slipped underneath her chin and Olivia found herself looking into his blue eyes once again.

"I can finish out the night," Bee said, and his lips hovered only an inch away from hers. "One last dance under the sheets before it all ends."

Olivia shook her head. "I think I just want to close my eyes and sleep," she told him, and then added, softly, "will you play it again?"

Bee smiled down at her and kissed her forehead.

"Anything for you, mama," he said against her skin. He took her hand again and the song repeated on the radio.

Olivia rested her head against his chest again, but she kept her eyes open this time. There was a picture of Harold on the China cabinet near her kitchen table, handsome and young in his Navy uniform, and she kept her eyes on that picture until her world faded into darkness with the chorus of their song.

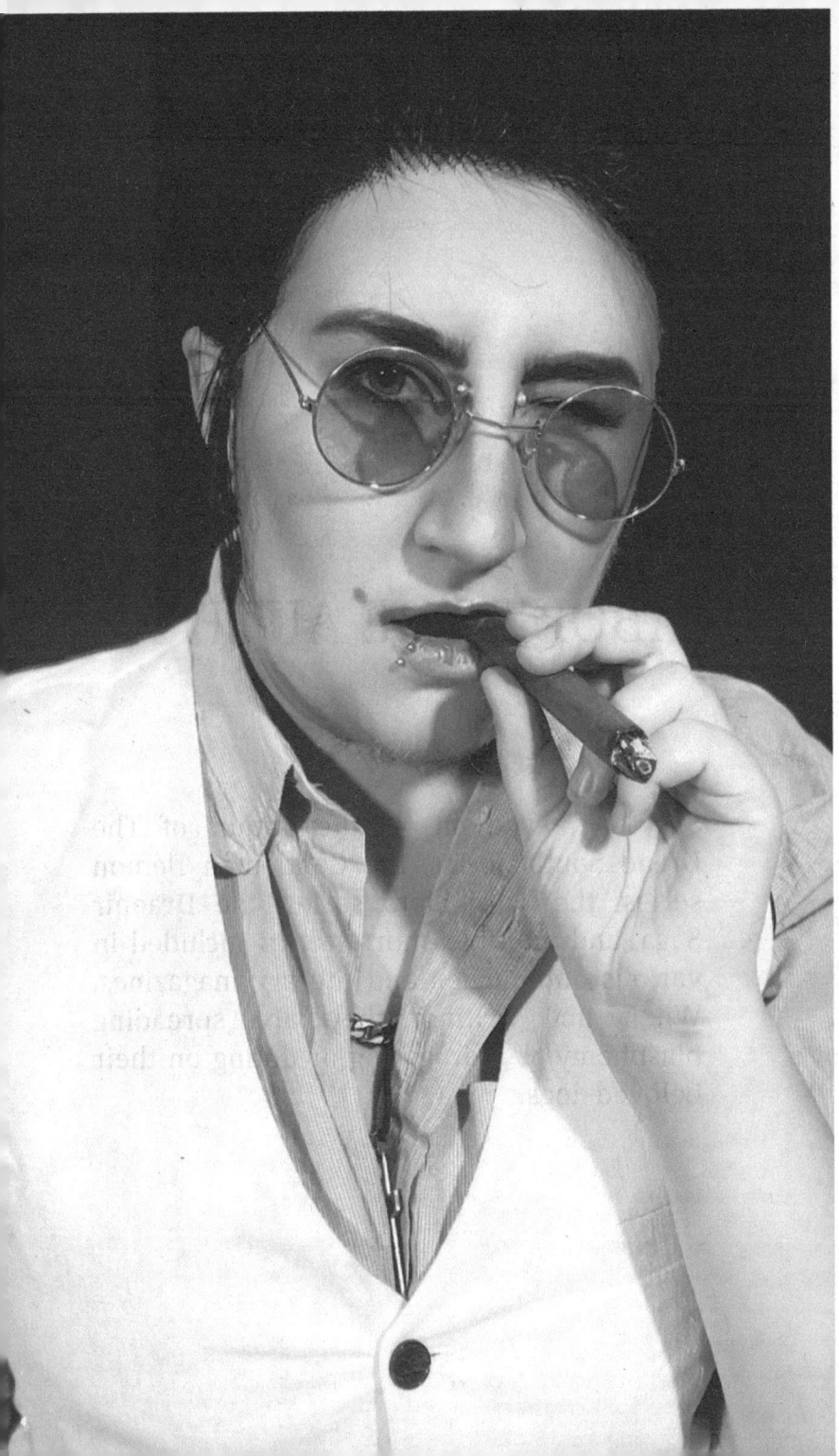

ABOUT THE AUTHOR

SIRIUS (they/them) is the author of The Dread South Series, the Gentleman Demon series, the Wirekillers series, the Draonir Saga, and multiple short stories included in various anthologies and literary magazines. When not writing, they are spreading blasphemy as a drag king or doting on their beloved dogs.